To Hold a Lady's Secret

Heart of a Duke

USA TODAY BESTSELLER

CHRISTI CALDWELL

To Hold a Lady's Secret
Heart of a Duke Series

Copyright © 2020 by Christi Caldwell

All rights reserved. No part of this book may be reproduced in any form by any electronic or mechanical means—except in the case of brief quotations embodied in critical articles or reviews—without written permission.

The characters and events portrayed in this book are fictitious. Any similarity to real persons, living or dead, is purely coincidental and not intended by the author.

This Book is licensed for your personal enjoyment only. This Book may not be re-sold or given away to other people. If you would like to share this book with another person, please purchase an additional copy for each recipient. If you're reading this book and did not purchase it or borrow it, or it was not purchased for your use only, then please return it and purchase your own copy. Thank you for respecting the hard work of the author.

Content Warning: Mentions of Sexual Assault

For more information about the author:
www.christicaldwellauthor.com
christicaldwellauthor@gmail.com
Twitter: @ChristiCaldwell
Or on Facebook at: Christi Caldwell Author

For first glimpse at covers, excerpts, and free bonus material, be sure to sign up for my monthly newsletter!

Printed in the USA.

Cover Design and Interior Format
© THE KILLION GROUP INC.

Other Titles by Christi Caldwell

HEART OF A DUKE
In Need of a Duke—Prequel Novella
For Love of the Duke
More than a Duke
The Love of a Rogue
Loved by a Duke
To Love a Lord
The Heart of a Scoundrel
To Wed His Christmas Lady
To Trust a Rogue
The Lure of a Rake
To Woo a Widow
To Redeem a Rake
One Winter with a Baron
To Enchant a Wicked Duke
Beguiled by a Baron
To Tempt a Scoundrel
To Hold a Lady's Secret

THE HEART OF A SCANDAL
In Need of a Knight—Prequel Novella
Schooling the Duke
A Lady's Guide to a Gentleman's Heart
A Matchmaker for a Marquess
His Duchess for a Day
Five Days with a Duke

LORDS OF HONOR
Seduced by a Lady's Heart
Captivated by a Lady's Charm
Rescued by a Lady's Love
Tempted by a Lady's Smile
Courting Poppy Tidemore

SCANDALOUS SEASONS
Forever Betrothed, Never the Bride
Never Courted, Suddenly Wed
Always Proper, Suddenly Scandalous
Always a Rogue, Forever Her Love
A Marquess for Christmas
Once a Wallflower, at Last His Love

SINFUL BRIDES
The Rogue's Wager
The Scoundrel's Honor
The Lady's Guard
The Heiress's Deception

THE WICKED WALLFLOWERS
The Hellion
The Vixen
The Governess
The Bluestocking
The Spitfire

THE THEODOSIA SWORD
Only For His Lady
Only For Her Honor
Only For Their Love

DANBY
A Season of Hope
Winning a Lady's Heart

THE BRETHREN
The Spy Who Seduced Her
The Lady Who Loved Him
The Rogue Who Rescued Her
The Minx Who Met Her Match
The Spinster Who Saved A Scoundrel

LOST LORDS OF LONDON
In Bed with the Earl

BRETHREN OF THE LORDS
My Lady of Deception
Her Duke of Secrets

REGENCY DUETS
Rogues Rush In: Tessa Dare and Christi Caldwell
Yuletide Wishes: Grace Burrowes and Christi Caldwell
Her Christmas Rogue

STANDALONE
Fighting for His Lady

MEMOIR: NON-FICTION
Uninterrupted Joy

PROLOGUE

Twelve years earlier
Cheshire, England

"I HATE BOYS."

That made two of them.

Boys were miserable little buggers. And the more powerful they were, the meaner they were, too. They delighted in making a person feel bad about oneself. That inexorable truth was the reason that Colin Lockhart now found himself hiding in a copse.

"Are you listening, Colin?" The beleaguered voice came from over by the brook, where Lady Gillian Farendale gathered stones and dropped them into her basket.

He peeked about before speaking. "Yes, I heard you." The problem was, anyone looking for Colin was likely to hear her, too.

He should have known better than to not answer her. She hated silence with the same burning intensity the sun hated the English sky.

"You didn't say anything," Gillian chided. "You know, you are very distant today. It is not at all like you."

Actually, it was very much like him... with everyone except the chattering girl he called a friend.

Gillian paused in her rock collecting to throw the back of a hand to her forehead in her not-unfamiliar dramatic manner. "I'm never going to get married."

"Of course you are," he said under his breath as he once more ducked his head out from behind the enormous tree trunk. Colin searched about for his latest nemeses. "Ouch," he grunted as his leg crumpled beneath him. He turned a sharp glare over his shoulder at the one responsible for the well-aimed rock to the backside of his knee. "What in the devil was *that* for?"

"Because you don't get to say whether or not I'm going to get married." With a little toss of her blonde curls, Gillian bent and collected another rock from the brook. She held it aloft and eyed it for several moments before adding it to her basket.

"What is with your sudden interest in rocks?" he asked, unable to help the question.

"It's not so very sudden." She shrugged. "They're pretty and useful, and one never knows when one will require a good rock."

He snorted. "A *good* rock?" Rocks weren't going to put food on a table, and they certainly weren't going to warm a cottage.

"Do you have a problem with my collection?"

That arch tone had him instantly schooling his features. When presented with either an impending battle with Layton Langley or a match against Gillian, Colin would choose the former every day of the week. "Of course not."

"Well, that is good, because I'm still cross with you for trying to marry me off to any old gentleman." She plunked another rock into her rapidly increasing collection.

Given he was risking a beating if discovered in his current hiding spot, it really wasn't prudent to engage in his customary discussions and debates about... anything with Gillian. Not this time. People were looking for him, and Colin wasn't one to lose at anything, including a confrontation with Cheshire's biggest bullies. Even with all that, he'd never been able to let it go with her. "I didn't say 'any old gentleman.' He could be a young one."

She glared at him. "Are you making light?"

"Gillian, you are the daughter of a marquess." This time as he delivered those words, he was wise enough to keep watch on Gillian, her basket... and his leg.

Her eyes formed tiny little slits. "And?" she prodded, planting her hands on her hips. The basket hung awkwardly at her side.

"And? You aren't dim, Gillian." In fact, she was the cleverest person he knew. "Noblemen's daughters marry other noblemen's sons. That's... just the way. Now, if you'd just go?" They were going to find him. With all this noise and all this chattering, discovery was inevitable. There was also the matter of her father, who'd spoken to Colin's mother about not wanting her bastard son being friendly with his proper daughter. "We can play later."

Gillian wasn't deterred. "It doesn't have to be the way you describe. I don't have to marry a nobleman."

Yes, yes, she did. He opted this time, however, to let the matter go.

"Furthermore," She flung another exaggerated hand over her brow. "No one is going to want to marry me."

He scrutinized her with a new and even deeper degree of wariness. This was dangerous territory. Colin knew next to nothing about little girls, but he knew this had all the makings of a trap. "You..." *Oh, blast*. What was he supposed to say here? Colin spoke on a rush. "You don't know that." There! He'd—

By the angry little sparkle in her eyes, those had not been the words she'd been in search of.

He fiddled with the frayed collar of his ancient jacket and tried again. "And... why wouldn't they want to marry you? You're—"

Gillian arched forward on the balls of her feet. "*Yesss?*" She stared expectantly at him.

For a moment, he thought she might have been fishing for compliments, because surely she knew why she was the only girl he preferred in the whole damned countryside.

"And you're clever. You spit farther than anyone I know. You can deliver a nasty blow to a person a stone bigger than you." And if those weren't reasons enough that a boy shouldn't want to marry a girl? Well, then, he didn't know what else to say.

Gillian sank back on her heels. "My father said I was flighty."

"Your father doesn't have a brain between his ears." That hateful nob, who, when he wasn't inviting illustrious guests only to raise his prestige, was sending his servants with orders for Colin to stay away from Gillian.

Gillian's eyes lit, bright and clear, and so *something* that he squirmed, unnerved by that show of emotion. That was certainly *not* the kind of relationship he had with Gillian.

"That is what my sister Genevieve is forever saying."

"Well, she's right," he said distractedly, stealing another peek out from behind his hiding space. They weren't going to quit until they found him. And with Gillian's usual chattering, it would be only a moment before they discovered them... or, more specifically, Colin. "Gillian, I've got company I'm expecting."

He might as well have stolen her bait for the wounded look she gave him. "You... have new friends?"

No. She was the only one. The only one he'd ever had, in fact. Admitting as much, admitting that he was facing another beating, however, proved one admission he couldn't make to even his best friend. "Would you mind?" he asked impatiently.

Gillian folded her hands primly. "Not at all."

Except, she made no move to leave.

"What are you doing?" he blurted.

"You were asking me to greet your new friends, were you not?"

New friends. He silently scoffed. That was one way to describe Langley, MacArthur, and Meadows. "No," he said bluntly. "I was certainly not."

Her face crumpled. "Oh."

And damned if he didn't feel like he'd just kicked a cat for the wounded glimmer in those eyes that revealed too much. Even so, he needed her gone.

Now.

Gillian sighed. "Very well. I shall leave you to your friends." She took two steps, swinging her basket as she went, and then wheeled back to face him. "Is it that they're boys and you are tired of hanging out with a girl after all these years?"

He swallowed a groan. Good hell. This was not the time for this. "*Of course* not."

Those three words, however, didn't suffice. "Because I am not like a *girl* girl." No, she wasn't. "I ride astride, and we hunt, even though I don't like hunting." Her eyes widened. "Is that what it is?"

"Gillian?" he said impatiently.

By the crestfallen look that stamped her features, she'd been expecting more. "Hmph." With that little grunt, she adjusted the small basket of stones. "Very well, I'll leave you to them." With a toss of her blond curls, she left.

Finally. Now he could—

"There he is."

Colin cursed. His heart pounded hard and loud in his ears, and he took a step to flee.

Too late.

"Got you, you miserable bastard."

The two boys behind the leader of the trio dissolved into laughter, as if the cleverest insult had been dealt, rather than a mere statement of fact about Colin's birthright.

His feet twitched. Colin longed to run, and yet... He was many things. Illegitimate. Sometimes surly. But he wasn't one who'd back down when confronted by his bullies. Still, when Colin stepped out from his hiding spot, his stomach sank.

Lord Langley and two of the sons of some landed gentry stood shoulder to shoulder. All in equal states of flawless dress. From their wool tailcoats on down to their gleaming, buckled boots, they were the model of privilege and power and... everything Colin was not.

"I don't have any problems with you," Colin called, proud of how even his voice was when inside he was shaking. It wasn't that each boy was particularly strong, but when they combined forces? He suppressed a shudder.

Bulky Lord Langley looped his thumbs into his strained waistband and ambled over. He stopped three feet away from Colin. "Yes, that might be true, but you see, we have problems with you."

Three feet. The distance was close enough to pounce and close enough that Colin couldn't escape without the other boy landing at least one blow. But it was always more than one. Particularly as he had his lackeys with him.

Colin brought his arms up, folding them close at his chest, so he was in position to counter any strike. "Oh? Am I supposed to guess what offense I've supposedly committed *this time?*"

"We saw you talking to Lady Gillian Farendale again," Benny MacArthur interjected as he leaned around Langley.

Langley glared at the small, slender boy.

MacArthur instantly fell back.

When Langley faced Colin, his dark look was reserved once more for Colin. "We saw you and the youngest Farendale girl," Langley confirmed, as if he required the pleasure of that reveal. "You've no place speaking to a lady."

No, Colin didn't. But he'd be damned if he let these village bullies to the decision. "There's no crime in speaking to a lady." And he was familiar with crime and law. Studying those books Gillian sneaked from her father's library was how he spent his nights.

"It should be." Langley flashed a slightly yellowed, gap-toothed smile. "After all, your mother is a whore."

Hatred snapped through Colin, and it was all he could do to maintain his restraint to keep from pouncing on and pounding the other boy. There was one certainty, however: There'd be no getting out of it this day, then. "My father is a duke," Colin pointed out. "And you're only just a baron's son, so?" He lifted his shoulders in a shrug. "And not even by blood."

"It is by blood," Langley shouted. "You don't know what you're talking about."

The fact that he and his family had come to their title by a chance twist of fate was Langley's weakness. Rumors said the boy's family had never even met the ancient baron from whom they'd received the title.

If Colin were a better person, he'd stop baiting Langley. But Colin wasn't a better person. A fight was certain, and if he was going to have it, Colin would also have the other boy unsettled. Colin tapped his chin in feigned contemplation. "Was there blood between you and the last baron, though? A third cousin twice removed died?" He looked to the other boys, who scratched at deeply puzzled brows.

Langley caught the confusion from his pair and thumped his fist against MacArthur's arm. "Stop it. There's a blood connection."

"Of course," MacArthur and Meadows said in obedient unison, compliant, loyal friends once more.

Langley approached; his hulking frame bent and poised for battle. "I'm going to end you, Lockhart."

Letting out a roar, Colin charged. His own frame, however, was slighter compared to the other boy's bulk, and Langley cuffed him in the face, knocking Colin to the ground.

Colin landed hard and all the air in his lungs left him on a whoosh. Giving his head a clearing shake, he braced as Langley came for him once more. He waited, timing his kick so that it was just right. Until Langley stood over him, and smiled coldly back.

Colin braced; preparing to kick the bigger boy between the legs.

"Owww," Langley cried out, and spun around.

What in hell? Colin scrambled to stand.

A small rock hit Langley squarely between the eyes.

The village bully squealed like a stuck pig. Tears immediately sprang to the boy's eyes as he rubbed at the red and rapidly swelling mark.

Colin's eyebrows went flying up as he looked from the first, sizable stone that had hit the boy, to the one responsible for that blow.

Gillian stood there, her hands on her little hips and anger blazing from her eyes. Even as diminutive as she was at just a handful of inches past four feet, Colin found himself as unnerved by her ferocious presence as the trio cowering off to the side. "Who do you think you are, Layton Langley?" she shouted.

"I'm a—"

"Don't go, 'I'm-a-baron's-son-and-one-day-a-baron'ing,' me, Layton Langley," she cut in. "You're nothing but a bully and a coward."

The boy's cheeks went all the redder, and he swiped the back of his sleeve over his nose, which was dripping with snot.

Gillian, however, wasn't done with them. She whipped about to face his partners in crime. "And what do you think your mother would say to you, Benny MacArthur?" She spun to the smallest of the trio, cowering at MacArthur's side. "Or you, Terry Meadows? Do you think she'll be proud to find out that you're being nothing but a big bully?"

Both boys, properly chastised, dropped their gazes to the ground.

"Now"—she stomped over—"get going." When they didn't immediately leave, Gillian clapped her hands once.

That sprang two of the boys into movement. In their haste to flee, both tripped and stumbled into each other before taking off in opposite directions. Then only Langley remained.

"As for you, Langley, I've little doubt that your own bully of a father won't care much what trouble you find yourself up to. You're just like him." She peered down the length of her pert little nose at him in a spectacular display of disdain better suited to Gillian's powerful mother, Lady Ellsworth.

Langley's bulging Adam's apple moved wildly, and then he found his footing. "I am just like my father, but you, Gillian Farendale? You are nothing like your proper, respectable mother and father. You're trash." Langley's voice climbed. "Trash, just like he is. And someday, you are going to find yourself in trouble because of the company you—"

Gillian let fly another stone.

"—keep—*ahh*."

The missile connected solidly with the boy's nose.

The appendage immediately fountained forth a crimson cascade.

Covering his entire face with his hands, Langley blubbered and sobbed. "You *broooooke* it," he wailed. And then, with blood pouring through his fingers, the stocky boy went racing off. All the while screaming for his mother.

Until... there was quiet once more.

Gillian dusted her palms together. "I never thought he'd leave," she muttered. As if she'd already forgotten the horrible words hurled at her by the gathering of boys, she turned a beaming smile upon Colin. "And here you said there was no such thing as a 'good' rock."

"I didn't need you to save me, Gillian."

Lifting the hem of her white skirts, she picked her way daintily

To Hold a Lady's Secret

along an uneven path of large rocks, playing like the young girl she was and not the heroic defender who'd just sent the ugliest brutes in the village running. "I didn't save you," she said conversationally, tossing her arms out to balance herself when she almost tipped off her perch. "If I *had* saved you, you wouldn't be sporting that enormous bruise."

Colin's fingers flew to that forgotten injury. He winced. His mother would see and ask questions, and he'd have to again lie and insist it had nothing to do with her, when it had everything to do with her.

Hiking her skirts higher, Gillian hopped onto dry ground and skipped over. "Let me see."

"It is fine," he insisted, but she already had him by the hand and was dragging him toward the small stream.

She pointed to a nearby boulder. "*Sit.*"

The power of her birthright brought him swiftly onto his buttocks, rushing to comply. She probed and prodded the swelling lump.

He flinched.

"Those terrible, terrible boys." Her eyes glinted with anger. "Hurting you as they did."

His lips twitched in his first smile of the morn. "You are in need of better insults."

"Langley's a gibface blunderbuss." Gillian tore the hem of her skirts. "A regular old bull calf."

"That is better." He eyed her movements as she soaked that delicate lace. Her mother was going to have her head for that affront to her dress.

Only, she wasn't done verbally tearing down Langley. "He's a corny-faced flapdoodle."

He strangled on his swallow. "A fl-flap—"

"You know," she cut him off. "A flapdoodle." She lifted up her smallest finger. "His naughty bits."

"*I* know what a flapdoodle is," Colin said on a rush. His cheeks fired hot. The question was how did she? He, however, had no intention of wandering down that path of discussion with her.

"And that is why I'm never going to marry. That is how all

noblemen are."

"It's not how they *all* are," he said automatically.

She paused in her probing and gave him a look. "Aren't they, Colin? *Aren't they?*" She placed a slight emphasis on those two words the second time she spoke.

He scrunched up his brow. It was certainly how his father, the randy Duke of Ravenscourt, was. And it was also how her ruthless, miserable father was. And Langley and his father. Yes, mayhap she was correct, after all. "I... I don't know, Gillian. There has to be a good one among the bunch."

"I shan't marry them, Colin," she said, her voice shaking. "I shan't do it."

"Well, you can't marry all of them. Just one."

That weak bid at humor fell flat.

She glared at him. "Are you making light *again*?"

"As it is, you have many, many years before you have to worry about it, Gillian. I'm certain some good nobleman will come along in that time."

"That is highly doubtful," she muttered.

And he was forced to agree with her... albeit silently.

"There is only one choice that makes sense."

"Oh?" He eyed her warily. After all, nothing really made sense where Gillian Farendale was concerned.

"If I do not find a good, honorable man to marry by the time I'm twenty-three, then we shall marry."

Him? Marry... her? Or, for that matter, marry anyone? "You're assuming *I* won't be married by twenty-three," he pointed out, hedging.

Gillian pointed her eyes at the tree overhead. "Of course you won't. You don't like girls."

Yes, well, she had him there. Or that had been the case. Recently, he'd begun noticing... things about girls that he didn't like himself for noticing. Details about their bosoms and other wicked thoughts that reminded him that he was like the dishonorable duke who'd sired him.

He shifted uncomfortably. "Geez, I don't know, Gillian. There has to be a good one among the bunch."

"And if there *isn't?*" she whispered. "What then?"

What then? She'd still find herself comfortable and secure, which was a good deal more than Colin's own mother knew.

"I was thinking we might also have a *Mariage Grand Cirque.*"

That brought Colin back to the moment. "A...*what?*"

"It is French for," she said punctuating the air with her two index fingers, as if that would somehow help him translate that foreign language. "A Grand Marriage Circus. Animals don't have to be there, if you don't want." Her eyes lit. "But perhaps they *shall?* And there'll be games and archery and—"

"I don't want a grand-wedding-anything, Gillian," he said, impatiently cutting her off. "And...And...even if I *did*..." He wouldn't. "We don't have any other real friends to invite." There was no disputing *that.*

Gillian appeared stricken, and just as he began feeling badly for hurting her, she brightened. "But perhaps someday we'll have a very many friends, and—"

"No." To all of it: to the false idea that there'd be more than he already knew or had for family and *friends.* To the wedding circus. To the damned wedding.

She sighed. "Oh, very well."

A cry went up. "Gilliaaaan!"

Oh, bloody hell. Someone was searching for her.

Nay... Colin strained his ears. Not just... anyone.

"Gillian Farendale?"

Gillian's always brightly colored cheeks faded white. "Oh, dear." The father.

It was a dire day indeed if the lazy, portly, and highly inactive marquess went out searching the countryside for Gillian. Even Colin knew that. Only... it would also be a good deal worse for Colin. Springing into movement, Colin gripped her by the shoulders, ringing a gasp from her.

"Colin!" she whispered.

"You have to go," he said frantically. For her. But especially for him. If he was discovered with the marquess's daughter... Sweat popped out on his brow.

"But our arrangement, Colin."

Colin tossed his hands up. "We don't *have* an arrangement, Gillian."

"Giillllian, where are you?" The marquess's calls grew increasingly closer.

"That is my point," she said calmly. "I cannot leave until it is settled." Gillian spit into her palm and extended that saliva offering to him.

He blanched. "What in blazes—?"

There came the crack and crunch of brush and twigs breaking under the noisy approach of the marquess. And because he would have offered her anything to get her gone and save himself from discovery and her father's ire, Colin spit into his own hand and placed it in hers. "I'll marry you if you don't find a good fellow by—" He released her quickly.

"Twenty-three," she said, entirely too loud.

"Fine. Fine." It was a lifetime away, and even when she reached those years, she'd be married. "Twenty-three." Again taking her by the shoulders, this time more firmly, he pushed her in the direction of her father's approaching voice.

"Do you promise?" she asked, seeming wholly unworried about the prospect of discovery.

But then, Colin was the one facing hell and trouble if they were caught together. "Didn't I just shake your hand?" *Please, go!*

She smiled. "Splendid. I'll draw something up and bring it for you to sign—"

"*Gillian.*"

"Oh, fine."

With their deal struck, she thankfully took herself off, saving him from discovery by her father.

CHAPTER 1

LADY GILLIAN FARENDALE HAD EITHER been trapped… or caught.

She'd gone back and forth over which it was since that hated carriage, and the even more hated occupant of that carriage, had descended some thirty minutes ago.

And in reflecting, as *caught* meant there was no escape, she vastly preferred *trapped*.

After all, a trap suggested there was also a way out.

And there had to be.

Because the alternative… was not one she'd allow herself to consider.

"I shouldn't have said anything," Mildred whispered for the tenth or so time since she'd come flying into Gillian's chambers to share word of the *gentleman's* arrival. The gleaming windowpane reflected the young maid's agonized features. "I… just thought I might mention he was here, and according to several of the parlor maids, your name was overheard."

The front door opened, and a figure stepped out. Adjusting his ridiculously high D'Orsay hat, the gentleman took the steps to his carriage jauntily. Triumphant. That was what they were. After four weeks of turning him away and rejecting his calls for marriage, he'd come here to rob her of choice. Fury had a taste, and it was sharp like vinegar on her tongue. "Oh, no," she said, letting the curtain fall so she didn't have to look upon his hated figure. "You can rest assured I'm grateful to you for telling me." In doing so, Mildred, along with the other maids, had allowed Gillian some time to prepare.

And yet, was there really any way to prepare for whatever was to come?

Gillian began to pace. This moment had been inevitable. From the moment she'd stolen out with her friend Honoria Fairfax for one of impolite society's most scandalous affairs and made the mistake of wandering off with a rake and sipping the champagne he'd given her, this threat had loomed.

It couldn't be enough that the scoundrel had taken what he'd no right taking, now he'd try to trap her into marriage?

The window, left slightly ajar by her maid, sent a light breeze filtering into the room, stirring the curtains and allowing Gillian a glimpse of the aged carriage as it lurched into motion and rolled off.

Perhaps the visit had nothing to do with her. Perhaps it had been gentlemanly business or Parliamentary affairs—

Between Society's darkest rake and your father? a voice jeered.

She winced. Yes, unlikely.

A scratching sounded at the door, and as one, she and Mildred turned to face the doorway.

Well, there was the end of the possibility that the visit wasn't about her.

Oh, God. How much had he revealed? Because there could be no doubting that, with the viscount's insistent attempt to marry her, he'd revealed something. Any detail would be enough to horrify.

Scratch-scratch-scratch.

"My lady," one of the maids called hesitantly from the other side. "Your presence is requested below by the marquess and marchioness."

Her stomach lurched. Oh, this was bad. Very, very bad indeed.

Gillian remained there, unmoving.

"I can say you've gone out, my lady," the young girl whispered.

For one very brief moment, Gillian considered the offer. She thought of taking the coward's path, onward and away from the meeting waiting to unfold below… with her father.

But she was no coward.

"Thank you, Mildred," she murmured. "It is fine." Which was one of the greatest understatements she'd made in the course of her twenty-four years. As Gillian made her way from the room, the servant looked on the cusp of tears.

Gillian herself wasn't a crier. She never had been.

But if ever there was a situation for a good, hearty weeping, this was decidedly that moment. A short while later, she found herself outside her father's offices.

She lifted her hand to knock, but paused in midmotion. To knock would put her at a disadvantage. It would establish roles in the conversation that was to come, where she was subservient to her father. And she was sick to death of that.

Clasping the handle, she pressed it, letting herself in.

Her parents' gazes, dripping vitriol and disgust—so very different than their usual, and much preferred, apathy—met hers. There was plenty of silence, too.

All her bravado and courage flagged.

They had found out her secret. As she'd suspected, it had been inevitable. She'd been a fool to expect her parents would not have found out. One of the most ruthless gossips in Society, the Marchioness of Ellsworth, could have pulled the secrets from the Home Office before the war office had even realized they'd been breached. Gillian, however, had not imagined it playing out this way—with Lord Barber outing her to her parents.

"Father," she said calmly. "Mother."

"Shut the door, Gillian," her mother snapped.

Just like that, she was the same scared girl who'd gone out of her way to avoid her cold, unfeeling, and always disapproving parents. Gillian pushed the door shut behind her.

Resisting the urge to move under the weight of those fierce gazes, she kept her arms forcibly at her sides, refusing to be cowed. Refusing to be broken by her parents.

And certainly not by the cad who'd taken his leave.

Gillian lifted her chin in silent defiance and waited. Forcing them to begin the conversation.

Her father jabbed a finger at the vacant seat opposite his desk, ordering her about without even the benefit of words.

Why, he'd show greater respect for his damned hunting dogs.

When she didn't immediately comply, her father's arm wavered and then fell. "*Sit.*"

"I'd rather not."

Her mother gasped. "Gillian, listen to your father this instant."

"I did," she said coolly. "His was a question, asking me to join him, and mine was an answer saying I've no desire to." She turned to go.

"That was not a question. It was a command. You are not to leave this room. I'm ordering you to remain."

She could leave. They couldn't force her to remain. Not really. But the exchange would eventually have to happen, and she was eager to have it done.

Making a slow march over to the cognac-colored swivel library chair vacant next to her mother, Gillian made herself sit.

She directed her eyes over the top of her father's balding pate to the painting just behind him. A girl in enormous frothy pink and white skirts sailed high in her swing, her toes kicked out and her slipper flying through the air. It was a piece she'd never understood. Not because of its beauty—there could be no doubting that—but rather, that lightness and joyfulness so at odds with the emotionally deadened man who'd sired her. A man who, when he'd discovered Gillian in a near identical replication of that scene he'd hung so near to him, had boxed her ears for doing something as uncouth as playing upon a swing.

Her father broke the silence. "Well, do you have nothing to say?"

Gillian made herself tear her gaze from the heeled slipper upon the canvas and looked in her father's general direction.

He'd asked the same question in the same tone when she'd first made friends with Honoria and Phoebe. *Scandalous women, the lot of them,* her parents frequently said. They also blamed them for her lack of serious suitors. *And also years earlier, when you befriended... Colin Lockhart.*

Colin, a friend so loyal and devoted he'd fought the village bullies beside her and—

"She's not saying anything." The marchioness looked from her husband to her daughter and then back again. "Why isn't she saying anything?"

Eager to have this concluded—her secret was at last exposed, so she might come right out and reject Lord Barber's request—she arched an eyebrow. "Perhaps you might be so good as to educate me as to what my latest sin is, Mother?"

"Oh, you know," her mother whispered. "You know*ww.*"

Her heart slipped into her stomach and sent it roiling with nausea. Oh, God. *How* much had he revealed? She'd not allowed herself to consider that when his carriage had rolled up… because if he were to reveal all the details of her shame that night, then he'd also be laying himself bare to a like shame. She'd still not accepted that dastards weren't capable of feeling shame.

Her father clapped his hands. "You may speak now."

He'd taken her silence as an indication of obedience. A panicky laugh built in her chest. "Oh, I'd raaather not." Nor would she play at this fishing expedition for information they might or might not be partaking in.

Her mother sat upright. "I'll begin, then. Lord Barber paid a visit."

"And what does that have to do with me?" she hedged, buying whatever time she might.

Her mother pounced, springing forward in her seat and hissing like a cat. "What were you *thinking* going to that… that… ball?"

Her gut churned all the more.

And there it was. Confirmation of what she'd known they'd likely discovered, but had hoped they hadn't. "It wasn't *really* a ball." Not really. Not in any traditional, or even remotely traditional, sense. "More a masquerade?"

Couples had been kissing and caressing in the middle of the ballroom floor and then trading over to different, equally amorous dance partners. Even now, bile built at what she'd witnessed that night.

What had she been thinking indeed? Believing that scandalous affair would be adventurous and fun. Ironically, her memories of that night, following that sweet-tasting champagne, remained... blank. She recalled only shadows of moments beyond a sloppy kiss that she could not make out more of.

"Did you lie with him?"

Oh, God.

This... was too much.

What did a woman say when she knew what had transpired, but yet had no recollection of it either? She glanced past her mother's shoulder. How to say—to her or anyone—that, yes, but she'd no remembrance of the act. That the only reason she knew what happened was because of the sting of pain the following morn when she'd awakened in an unfamiliar parlor... with her skirts up and...

Her mind screeched to a stop.

"Say something!" her mother raged.

I cannot do this... I cannot think these things, let alone speak them, to my mother. "What is there to say?" Gillian managed, her voice weak. There was a scoundrel with whom she'd spent one night. The semantics of that, however, wouldn't save her. Whether it had been one time or one hundred times, the result had been the same.

At her silence, the marchioness looked over to her husband before looking once more to Gillian. "Deny it." Rage filled her mother's order. "Deny it," she said a second time, this time pleadingly.

Except... Gillian couldn't. And she wanted to throw up all over again, for reasons that had nothing to do with regret over the forgotten night she'd spent with Lord Barber.

Her mother tried once more. "*Please*, Gillian."

Refusing to give in to the swell of panic, especially here, before her parents, she continued to again concentrate on the jubilant lady on the swing. "I cannot do that," she finally said.

Silence marched on, marked by the incessant ticking of the clock, and as it did, her mother's skin went through a plethora of grays and whites, more shades than Gillian had known existed.

"Oh, my God," her mother whispered. "It is true." The marchioness wilted in her seat. For the first time in Gillian's life, the marchioness did that which she'd never before done—at least not in front of Gillian—she burst into tears.

Great, big, noisy, blubbering ones.

Tears she'd not even shed when Genevieve had lost her first babe.

Her father exploded from his chair. "He offered to do the right thing by you. Did he not?"

It was nothing personal. I just need your dowry.

She'd been a mark for a fortune hunter that night. "What is the right thing, really? Bed me, then wed me for nothing more than the money I bring?"

Her mother's gasp filled the room.

The marquess's fat lips moved, but there weren't any immediate words forthcoming.

In a world where men took mistresses and dallied nightly with different ladies and courtesans, women should be held to altogether different standards. They were shamed and ridiculed and disdained. And what was different? The men didn't have to worry about the consequences of those rendezvous.

The same could not, however, be said for women.

It was that indignation, safer and solidifying, that gave her strength to at last admit the secret that they would have ultimately discovered anyway.

"I'll not marry him." Oddly, there was something freeing in not having to hold on to that decision anymore. For weeks since that disastrous night, she'd lived with his specter following her. Telling him no, she'd not wed him, in every way. "I don't care what he said to you. I don't care what you think, or about the consequences." Of which there were many. "But I'll not tie myself to one such as him." It was as she'd said to Colin all those years ago: She'd never marry a damned nobleman—and certainly not a cad who'd sought to trap her.

Her parents gasped, two perfectly synchronous intakes of air.

"You'll…"

"Not," she finished for her father. "I said I will not marry Lord Barber."

He seethed, his eyes bulging and his cheeks flushing. "Your options, I fear, given the circumstances, are limited."

They were limited, but there… was one… Granted, he was one

who'd made a promise to her as a child, but, well, when one was desperate, one was desperate.

"I will not marry him," she said, coming to her feet. "You see, I am already betrothed."

Her father choked. "You are...?"

"Now, if you'll excuse me."

Taking advantage of their shock, Gillian hurried from the room and set to work on the business of finding a betrothed.

CHAPTER 2

WHEN COLIN LOCKHART, BASTARD-BORN SON of the Duke of Ravenscourt, had set out to build his own business as a detective, he'd thrilled at the prospect of choosing his assignments, and more… solving cases of import.

Not arresting boys and girls for filching the purses of some lords outside of Covent Garden. Not breaking up fights in the streets. But truly important cases.

Now, partner to his own investigative offices for two years now, he'd come to fully realize and accept that the cases were all the damned same.

That was, for people like him. Bastards. The fine lords and ladies took their help from people closer to them in rank.

Colin scanned the list of prospective clients requesting his services that his clerk had put together. There was work enough and, because of that, money enough, too.

That would be enough for most men.

But Colin wasn't most men. Since the moment he, his mother, and sister had been tossed out of Cheshire by the Marquess of Ellsworth, Colin had resolved to build himself into something. Something more than the bastard-born son of a duke who hadn't given two shites about his family on the side, or two farthings to support them.

Colin's hungering to be more, and have more, was born of a

desire to never again be that scared, penniless boy.

And yet, for the success he'd had as a private runner, that success had not followed him to his venture as a private detective. His clients remained more like him than the men and women who belonged to his father's elite ranks. As such, that so much more he craved continued to elude him, and for the very reasons he'd been shunned as a boy.

Licking the tip of his finger, Colin turned the page in his black leather journal, a gift from his sister some Christmases ago. All the while, he examined the potential list of clients his clerk had presented him with. All the respective names were people outside of the nobility, with but a handful of coins to pay, and yet, he also appreciated that those cases were no less important.

But he also had come to learn that they did not pay either.

Footfalls echoed outside his office. A moment later, his door opened.

"I'm working," he said by way of greeting, not even lifting his head.

"You're not solving a case. You're deciding on your next client," his partner, Mr. Roarke O'Toole, returned.

Frowning, Colin looked up. "I'd say the two are inextricably intertwined."

"Let me save you the benefit of your time and efforts. A handful of extortions, petty theft, and missing wives that don't want to be found, from people in East London." His partner quirked a brow. "Have I missed anything?"

Refusing to be baited, Colin shoved the folder close at his fingertips in the other man's direction.

"Those people also can't pay," O'Toole pointed out, coolly matter-of-fact.

"They can," he countered. Just not what he should be paid, or what Colin needed to build the business into everything he hoped for it. Having ventured out from the role he'd played as a most-celebrated runner, he'd never imagined anything but success for his own private business.

His friend gave him a look.

Colin's neck flushed.

"I have real work for you." A folder landed on his desk with a solid *thwack*.

Colin glanced up at O'Toole, then at the packet on his desk. He resisted a curse. "No," he said, before O'Toole could add anything more. He already knew what this was about.

His partner chuckled and, grabbing a chair, seated himself. "She didn't want my help."

She—none other than the old Countess Holderness—had all but set herself up as their personal proprietress. "I said no." He knew what the other man was going to say and what the old woman wanted.

"She pays a small fortune every time you solve a case for her. We don't have the luxury of simply rejecting those funds," his partner said bluntly.

They weren't cases. Not the kind that he'd committed himself to solving. Every time he went to see her, it was really about indulging an old woman who enjoyed his company. That was not why he'd thrown away his career for the prospect of having his own business. "I sent you."

"Yes, well, she turned me away. She *wants* you."

"To find her latest missing bauble?" He shoved back his chair and stood. "Tell her it's her lady's maid. It's been her lady's maid. And it will always be her lady's maid." And yet, for some unfound reason, the woman insisted on retaining the girl, and that was too bad. "My sole existence as an investigator isn't to cater to her personal desires."

"No," O'Toole said calmly. "It is important, however, to take work where work exists."

Colin's partner sighed. "Lockhart..." he began, and Colin knew precisely where the discourse was going. "I understand you don't want the assignment."

And he wasn't taking it.

"We need the work, and a substantial amount of it comes through our association."

Colin lifted an eyebrow "Your association with Lady Holderness."

"She quite likes you, she does."

"Catering to a seventy-year-old, lonely, bored noblewoman is not part of my job." Not the one he'd imagined, anyway. Frustration whipping through him, Colin grabbed for another file.

Roarke slapped a hand down on top of it. "It is when she's the reason we haven't had to shutter our doors and return to our previous work," his partner pointed out.

Guilt washed over him. For he'd been the one to persuade O'Toole, the second-best runner at Bow Street, to leave the security of that work and set out to create their own rival establishment.

They'd expected clients would follow, that their reputations would be enough to secure the work that had previously gone through Bow Street.

What neither he nor O'Toole had anticipated was just how powerful legacy was. People used that which they knew, what was comfortable. The Bow Street runners were established, and he and O'Toole had been inextricably intertwined with that organization. When they'd no longer been part of it, other men had simply stepped in to fill that void, and the public had continued to entrust their care to that age-old organization.

"It's fifty pounds, Colin," the other man said quietly. "Fifty pounds to speak to her."

Colin stared down at the folder, his pride as strong now as it had been in the village of Cheshire when he'd taken on the boys there.

But pride didn't see a belly filled or a family cared for. And since he'd taken on this venture, he'd had to rely on his brother Vail, the Baron Basingstoke, to help care for Catriona.

"Are you ready to talk about it?"

Colin stiffened. There it was, the debate his partner had raised a year ago. One that Colin had been resistant to engage in.

O'Toole dragged a chair closer to Colin's desk and sat. "Birmingham," he simply said.

He was already shaking his head. "We've already talked about Birmingham." Ad nauseam. "We decided—"

"You decided London had more opportunities because of the population of the nobility, yes, yes. But I'm not talking Babcary, I'm talking *Birmingham*." O'Toole spoke in a lower voice, placing a slight emphasis on that place in question. He didn't allow Colin a chance to edge a word in. "There's an investor there who wishes to meet you about the prospect of our moving our venture there."

"No."

O'Toole went on as if he hadn't spoken. "It's the second-largest city in England. A metropolis defined by its large population and shopping and theater and arts—"

"What are you? A damned Oxford instructor or an investigator?" Colin shut the journal Catriona had purchased for him for his last birthday.

His partner—and friend—flashed a wry grin. "I'm a man of reason who is trying to convince you to, if not at least consider the decision, to see logic in it."

"I have seen the logic," he said, "in staying here. To leave now would be to quit before we've really given ourselves the time to succeed." How could the other man not see as much?

"It's all that makes sense, Colin," his partner went on, returning to that same quiet insistence. "We cannot compete here."

"That's not true," Colin said through tight teeth. "We are the best at what we do." They had been. And they still would be. If they were presented with assignments where their skills could be properly put to use, then they'd gain the foothold they'd been trying to secure for the past three years now.

A sound of frustration left the other man. "Our skills don't matter if we aren't afforded the opportunities to use them. Just as our business can never have the fair shake because of our competition here." O'Toole dragged the chair closer and rested an elbow on the side of the desk. "We cannot have it the both ways you want it—money *and* the cases you seek for our business. Sometimes you have to choose."

And they were nearing the point where they had to.

O'Toole might as well have spoken the words out loud.

And yet, to leave would be to also leave behind the sister for whom he'd been responsible. The sister he'd had to leave in the care of his brother Vail, all while he'd set up his own business. If he left, he'd be leaving Catriona, as well as his found family, behind.

Leaving, as his father had done to pursue his own self-interests.

Wordlessly, O'Toole pushed Lady Holderness's file across the desk.

Tamping down a growl, he swiped the folder up and came to his feet. Colin started across the room.

"I'm not saying you have to take on her assignments," O'Toole called after him.

Connor yanked his cloak from the hook on the back of his door.

"I'm merely saying if you are unwilling to entertain moving our enterprise to Birmingham, well, then I can't really see an alternative other than taking on the lady's case."

No, the options were limited and the choices even fewer.

And he knew it. He didn't need O'Toole's reminder for it either.

They had to come to a decision about their agency… and it was one he wasn't yet ready to make.

CHAPTER 3

WHEN GILLIAN FARENDALE HAD BEEN a young girl, some of the village boys had called her trash and predicted she'd find herself in trouble for the company she kept.

And she discovered all these years later that Layton Langley, ironically, had been correct. Well, not about the trash part. She still didn't, wouldn't, and would never believe herself trash. But she had found herself in trouble.

Which was why she also found herself where she was now, where she'd been waiting for the better part of forty-five minutes. Pulling the deep hood of her cloak back a fraction, she consulted the clock hanging above the clerk's desk. Nearly an hour now.

The young, bespectacled man at work must have sensed her focus on that timepiece. "I've told you before, ma'am," he said, without bothering to pick up his head, "Mr. Lockhart is not expected to leave his office—"

"That is fine," she interrupted, drawing her hood back into back into place. "I'll wait." Or continue to wait, as the case might be.

With a grunt, the clerk resumed scribbling away in his book. Folding her hands, Gillian looked around at Colin Lockhart's sparse offices. But for the handful of row benches and chairs and the clerk's chair, there was a sterility to the rooms. Not that she much considered herself one for decorating and redecorating, but she could do a deal better than *this*.

As if he felt her assessing stare, the clerk lifted a disapproving frown.

She met that scowl with a smile.

"Hmph," he muttered and returned to his work.

Alas, if the annoyed young man wished to run her off with a disapproving look, he was destined to be disappointed. Between her mother and father, censorious glances were something Gillian had grown well accustomed to.

Of course, all their previous disappointments, however, would pale when presented with… this latest scandal.

Her stomach twisted, and she gripped the fabric of her black cloak.

Only… Was it really a scandal if no one knew about it? A panicky little giggle gurgled in her throat, earning yet another look from Mr. Angry Clerk. But she could not stifle the swarm of emotion. Scandals invariably came to light, and this was destined to be no different.

And in Gillian's case, there was nowhere else for her to turn. Not at this time, anyway.

She had a sister and brother-in-law away in the country, suffering through a complicated confinement. A friend in Phoebe, the Marchioness of Rutland who was abroad with her family. Another friend, newly married, Francesca, who would never turn Gillian away, but she certainly didn't need Gillian underfoot.

And there was of course, Honoria Fairfax. Honoria who'd been with her that night and whom Gillian had not been able to bring herself to face since. Because of the regret she carried. Because her friend had reservations before Gillian had convinced her to attend the masquerade…only to learn how very right the other woman had been.

And because of the shame. There was that, too.

Yes, she had those friends and knew they could and would listen and support her in anything and everything, but she couldn't go to them.

Gillian troubled her lower lip. Of course, Colin Lockhart was a friend, too. Granted, she'd not seen him in twelve years, and they'd both been children at the time, but it was easier not to think of the years between them. Nay, it was a good deal better to remember their friendship, which if one wished to be truly precise, had in fact been longer than all the other ones she had with the ladies she'd met and become closest with in London.

He, too, had been a friend, and as long as one thought in those terms, her seeking him out and being here and wanting to speak to him wasn't really all that unconventional.

Liar.

She wouldn't really be confiding in him. Not the full details. Only as much as she needed to say to secure what she required.

Those attempts to reassure herself didn't help.

She stole a look at his closed door. "Does he always work this long without interruption?"

"Yes," the clerk said automatically as he worked. He paused. "Not that it is your business to ask questions or mine to answer them about Mr. Lockhart."

Gillian resisted the urge to sigh and again consulted the clock.

When she'd rushed here, she'd imagined a rather quick meeting. Certainly not the lengthy wait that would allow her parents time with which to do whatever they intended to do next.

The door finally opened, and Colin stalked out.

At last.

Her heart sped up.

"Johnson," Colin greeted, all his focus on his clerk. "Do you have—?"

His clerk immediately jumped up. "I just completed them as you requested, Mr. Lockhart," he said, rushing over with the folder he'd been so busy working on during Gillian's time here.

Colin accepted the file and flipped through it.

Engrossed as he was, she used the moment to study him. Periodically over the years, she'd seen Colin at the most unexpected of places. The one mask-free figure at a masquerade. The casually clad detective being ushered through a ballroom before disappearing off with what could only be a client.

But she'd not seen him this close.

She'd not seen him… like this.

She'd always known she was wicked. Wickedness was, after all, what had brought her to this very point, but given the precarious state of her existence, one would think she'd be able to focus on her circumstances and not... him.

Alas, she was hopeless.

His hair was a little longer than fashion dictated, the dark strands framing the sharp planes of a face that had grown only more intriguing with time.

He was broader than she remembered. And taller and... everything. He didn't have the look of any of the gentlemen of Polite Society who either found themselves agonizingly slender or given to roundness. He was perfect in form and physique and... Crafted as a model of powerful male, he was... a stranger.

Stop it. This is Colin.

Colin, who had not been meeting with a client?

Craning her neck, she peered around him and his clerk. Why... why... he'd not been meeting with someone. "You were alone in there the whole time?" she blurted.

With a frown, Colin paused in talking with Mr. Johnson and looked over to Gillian. "Should I have been with someone?" he asked coolly.

"Well, given that I've been waiting to speak with you, it would have made me feel a good deal better to think you were with an actual person, Colin."

"Colin? What...?" Colin glanced questioningly to his clerk. "Who in blazes *is* this?"

Mr. Johnson made a clearing sound in his throat. "She has not said. She merely said she was here on a matter of import and insisted you'd wish to see her, and she refused to divulge her identity."

This? She?

Why, they spoke about her as if she were invisible. A nonentity. Given the miserable parents she had, it was not unfamiliar to be viewed that way, and yet, this time set her teeth on edge.

"I don't wish to see anyone who doesn't have an appointment, and I don't have any appointments," Colin was saying to his clerk with an air of finality, marking her time here at an end.

Over her dead body.

Color filled the younger man's cheeks, and he nodded. "I am

aware of your schedule, Mr. Lockhart. However, the young woman was not to be deterred."

Gillian pointedly cleared her throat. Both men looked over. "I assure you both, this will not take very long," she said, and without awaiting an invitation, she climbed to her feet and swept past the pair into Colin's office.

Her heart pounded as she passed the two men, more than half expecting to be grabbed by the back of her skirts and yanked out for that insolence.

The room was reflective of the waiting room: tidy, clean, and bare of all but a desk, chair, and a handful of storage cabinets. It was as perfunctory and no-nonsense as the man who'd just greeted her. Not that his had been much of a greeting.

Colin.

This is Colin.

The boy you played with and teased and tortured and…

She swallowed hard as he shut the door behind them. From under her hood, Gillian searched for some hint of that boy, but found nothing. He'd always been serious, and a frown had been more common than a smile from him, and yet, time had made him even more serious.

The harsh planes of his face lent an added layer of cynicism to him. Sharp cheeks. Hard, square chin. There'd been a dimple in his right cheek. Gillian's gaze searched—and found—that slight indentation. The one that proved he was more than cold, unyielding granite.

He filled the doorway, arms folded across his broad chest as his gaze bore into hers. "Let us be clear, I don't tolerate anyone invading my offices."

Well, that hadn't changed. He'd so loved the copse in Kent and had despised sharing it with anyone… except her. That hadn't been the case at first. When their paths had first crossed, he'd ordered her gone. In time, they'd struck up a friendship, and the memory of the bond they'd shared as children restored some of her flagging courage.

"Have I made myself clear?" He pushed away from the doorjamb, and she started.

Gillian managed a shaky nod. Mayhap she was just searching for glimpses of who they'd been in the past.

"Now, I'd suggest you come back at a later time when you have an appointment."

Gillian dug her heels in. "I'm not leaving."

He ran a gaze up and down her black cloak, lingering his focus briefly on the enormous hooding that shielded her face. "You're desperate."

He'd always been astute.

"I don't like to think of myself as desperate," she muttered under her breath. And yet—her heart clenched—that was what she was, wasn't it? It was why, in a brief moment of insanity, she'd come here to request a favor. Damn him for being altogether too astute.

Either way, a promise was a promise, and if she could secure his help, she would.

"A person who isn't desperate wouldn't show up without an appointment and insist on being heard out."

"Yes, well, that is true," she conceded. "But desperate also implies not having a choice. I had a choice to come to you or not. I'm choosing to be here and remain, despite the fact you'd rather I left."

"You require my services."

She cocked her head. Well, that was rather... blunt. Nor was he wrong. "Er... that is one way of thinking of it," she muttered as he came forward and set up a place behind his desk.

He didn't invite her to sit, a glaringly obvious omission on his part. "What was that?"

"Nothing." She, however, didn't need to wait for any polite offer from him. Taking the back of the curved oak chair, she pulled it out slightly and availed herself of the seat. Gillian folded her hands on her lap. "I take it you are accustomed to young women showing up in need of your... assistance?" she hedged, seeking time.

"My clients and those expecting to work with me know to set up a meeting," he said impatiently.

"Oh, I'm not a client." That wasn't what had brought her here. Rather, it had been desperation of a different sort.

"No, you're certainly not."

Oddly, those seemingly innocuous words sounded like a stiff rebuke.

As it was easier to focus on his rude treatment, she glanced to the door. "You know, you really should hire more-friendly staff."

His brows crept together. "I beg your pardon?"

"Your staff." She gestured to the doorway. "The gentleman, Mr. Johnson, out there? He was quite rude. I expect I might be of some help with that."

Miracle of miracles, Colin proved capable of more than a stern countenance. Confusion puckered his high brow. "I…"

"I can help you find staff who are clever, competent, and not rude." She glanced about his agency. "In fact, I might be of some assistance with the overall layout of your offices. A good deal of this set-up is not working because—"

"I assure you, the layout is just fine, and I don't require your or anyone's help in staffing matters." That drollness was the first glimmer of the mischievous, slightly sarcastic boy she remembered, and just like that, he comfortably restored them to the friendly pair they'd once been.

Gillian snorted. "Given Mr. Johnson? I would disagree and vigorously."

Colin's features instantly hardened.

So much for a truce, then.

Unnerved, she pushed her hood off and waited for the flash of recognition in Colin's greenish-brown eyes… that did not come. There was no shocked understanding. Or warm smile. When she'd imagined this playing out, there had at least been his half smile once she revealed herself to him.

"Who *are* you?" With that question, Colin confirmed what she'd already suspected.

Gillian glanced around the whitewashed plaster walls of Colin's offices. She'd had almost an entire hour to think about this exchange and what she'd say. In fact, she'd planned it all out on her journey here. She'd rehearsed it in the carriage. But all of it had been predicated on the belief that he would remember her. That his memories of their friendship would be as keen as her own. Only to learn, he had… no remembrance of her. Granted, she'd been a girl, but they'd known each other for twelve whole years. For the first time since she'd concocted her plan and come to him, her confidence flagged. This hardly proved promising.

"You don't recognize me," she murmured softly, the pang caused by that realization sharp and unpleasant in her breast.

He frowned. "Should I?"

"Yes," she said softly. "I rather think you should." For she recognized him. Some years back, when he'd been circulating in Lord Yardley's ballroom, she'd spied him among the crowd and knew him to be the friend from her past. "It is I…" She touched a hand lightly to her chest. "*Gillian.*"

The lines at the corners of his mouth deepened.

Oh, well, that was really quite enough. It was one thing to not recognize the sound of her voice or the sight of her face. But really, how many Gillians did he know? "*Gillian,*" she repeated, adding an extra syllable to her name in hopes that it would sink in.

He shook his head slowly, and then Colin froze. His lips parted in the slightest and only hint of a reaction that he remembered something about her. "*Lady* Gillian."

Lady Gillian?

The proper form of address was what he'd remember?

The lout.

He'd always been adamant that she was just Gillian to him, and she'd loved him for being a boy who'd not cared that her father was a marquess. She quirked an eyebrow. "Since when did you begin calling me Lady Gillian?"

"Since I grew up and you grew up, and I left Cheshire for London," he said flatly.

It appeared he'd lost the ability to identify when he was being teased. There were other things to wonder and worry after, but the fact that he'd been so transformed filled her with the keenest sadness.

"'I don't care if you're a princess or a pauper, you're just Gillian,'" she tossed back, the words from a long-ago time. Mayhap if he'd those reminiscences thrust before him, he'd be… more *Colin*.

His features proved implacable. "I trust you've not come here with the intent of debating or discussing how I do or do not refer to you?"

So he was all grown up and had added some surliness and cynicism to his years. They weren't unalike in that regard. Very well…

"No, you are correct. That is not why I've come." Bringing her shoulders back, she angled her chin up. Before her courage deserted her, she drew a breath and got to the sole reason for her being here. "You promised to marry me." Gillian smiled. Unfastening her cloak and letting it fall about her, she settled into her seat. "And I've come to officially accept."

CHAPTER 4

IN HIS WORK AS FIRST a Bow Street runner and then as an aspiring private investigator, Colin Lockhart had heard all manner of shocking statements, confessions, and revelations.

Women who'd admitted to killing their husbands, and who'd done so viciously, sharing each graphic detail of those murders.

Men who'd confessed the clever ways in which they'd fleeced longstanding business partners.

Not once had Colin been reduced to speechlessness.

That was… until now.

Of course Gillian Farendale would be the one to do it.

Gillian Farendale, whom he'd not seen in twelve years, though there were glimpses of her still, the pale blonde hair, the rounded cheeks. He slipped his detective's gaze up and down her person, lingering briefly on her full breasts. Her frame, however, was a woman's frame.

Colin gave his head a hard shake. Not, given her sudden reappearance and even more disturbing statement, that it mattered exactly how her form had changed.

"I know what you're thinking," she prattled on.

"No." Colin slowly shook his head. "I… don't think you do."

"You're thinking that we agreed to twenty-three," she went on, without seeming to require any contribution from Colin. "And I'm twenty-four, and as such, I'm a year late. You are not wrong."

Dumbfounded, he stared on as she fished around in her reticule and withdrew a folded sheet. Giving it several flourishing snaps, until the heavily creased, yellowed paper was open, she slapped it down on his desk.

"'If by the age of twenty-three, I remain unwed'"—Gillian's gaze remained locked with his as she recited words that had the quality of rote memorization—"'I, Gillian Farendale, do solemnly, soberly, and swearingly vow to take you, Colin Lockhart, as my respective husband.'"

Knocked off-balance, Colin looked down at that ancient-looking sheet, written in two different scrawls, both competing for most sloppy. "You… *saved* this?"

"'I, Colin Lockhart,'" she went on with her recitation, ignoring that question, "'do promise, vow, and commit myself to wedding you, if and only if you want it and if and only if you decide you want to. The decision will rest with you, but I promise I will. Even if I hate the idea of marriage, I will.'"

That was certainly something he had said, and all these years later, the declaration held firm and true.

Her ramblings continued. "'I do also promise that I shall not be mean or unkind…'"

She'd always had a wry, wicked sense of humor. She'd been cleverer than all the boys and girls in the village. And she'd teased and jested. Apparently, that remained unchanged.

Gillian finally finished her lengthy recitation. Silent at last, she folded her hands primly and waited.

Primly, his ass. There wasn't a prim thing about her. As if her being here, reminiscing about their past, wasn't proof enough of that. Alas, his life had become, and only was, his work. As such, if she'd sought him out to travel down memory lane with a friend from long ago, she'd sought out the wrong person. He'd neither the time, inclination, nor interest.

"Ahem." Gillian made a little clearing sound in her throat. "Well?"

Well? He shook his head.

Gillian gestured to that child's contract, and he followed her stare.

Then it hit him. Colin strangled on his spit, sputtering and choking. "Y-you—" All the while he struggled to squeeze words around his coughing fit, Gillian stared patiently back. "Y-you are *serrrious*."

"I am." Gillian held his gaze, her clear blue eyes piercing his. "Deadly so, Colin."

He choked on another swallow. "Are you… m-m—"

"Married? No," she said patiently, like schooling a child. "I've told you that is why I've come to you."

"—mad?" he at last got out, finally regaining control of his ability to breathe.

"Well, I'm not happy, if that is what you're asking. I'm quite affronted by your whole—"

"Insane," he snapped. Colin pointed at her head. "I'm asking if you've gone mad since I knew you."

Gillian bristled. "Of course not. And if I had, you shouldn't insult me at the expense of those individuals who are, in fact, not all right in the head."

She'd long been a champion for those deemed "lesser" or "different" by Polite Society. That was why, when they'd been children, she'd championed him.

And even as asinine as her explanation for being here, in fact was, it was because of the loyalty and devotion she'd once shown him, when all the world had only ever seen a bastard, that he couched his words. "I can't"—*won't*—"marry you."

The young lady went absolutely motionless. "You're married." Her lips barely moved as she spoke those two words.

"I am."

"You are?" she whispered. "I was so very certain…" Her face fell.

He should leave her to that conclusion she'd drawn. *If* he hadn't known her. *If* he'd trusted she'd leave and delve no further into his personal life. But given she'd sought him out all these years later proved she'd not ever do something as simple as take his proverbial word for it.

"To my work," he clarified. "I am wedded to my work. I don't have a wife." Nor, however, did he have any intention of saddling himself with one.

Relief marched across her face. "Oh, splendid," she said, apparently not having heard the first part of what he'd said. "Because I did read up on you and could find no mention of a wife, and I was certain that there would have been some indication somewhere had there been."

She, a marquess's daughter, had been reading up on him?

But then, none of this made sense. Least of all, her. Colin pressed his fingers against his temple.

"I know what you are thinking," she said.

"That you should stop with—"

"You worry about us having a true marriage. We don't have to be a real husband and wife," she promised.

He choked. By God, before this day was through, he was going to die of a conniption.

"I wasn't referring to the conjugal aspect of a marriage." Gillian pointed her eyes skyward. "My goodness, I'd not expected you should become squeamish at such talk."

She would come to his offices in the middle of his workday, unannounced and without an appointment. Take him from his work. Put some ludicrous, outlandish proposition of marriage based on a child's contract to him. And she'd sit there through it all with that aplomb and droll humor? Of course, that was how she'd always been. He'd simply let himself be thrown off-kilter. He was out of practice with the Lady Gillian Farendale.

In a display of nonchalance, Colin kicked back the legs of his chair. "Ohhh, I don't think conjugal relations means what you *think* it means, Gillian."

"No," she said bluntly. "I know precisely what I am talking about. Now, say I was referring to matters pertaining to the consummation of marital vows, I would have gone with the use of 'intercourse,' 'coitus,' or even 'sexual relations.'"

Colin's chair fell out from under him, and he toppled back, coming down hard. His entire neck and face went hot. Sprawled on the floor, with his chair the only cushion beneath him, he stared overhead at his office ceiling. *So much for turning the damned tables on the chit.*

Gillian stood so quickly, the legs of her own seat scraped along his planked floors. Those boards groaned as she came around his desk to stand over him. "Oh, dear, I've hurt you."

From outside, his clerk's footfalls came fast. "Mr.—"

"I'm fine," Colin shouted, shoving up onto his elbows.

"Are you certain—"

"I said I—"

"He most certainly is not fine," Gillian called over to the door. "I've rather hurt him."

There was a brief pause.

Oh, hell. Colin was still in the process of getting himself upright when Johnson tossed the door open. His loyal clerk's face blanched as Colin got himself to his feet. "My God, you are hurt."

"I told you as much," Gillian answered for him.

This was really enough. "Get the hell out unless you are called for."

All the color rushed back to Johnson's cheeks.

This time, the young man wisely took his leave, closing the door behind him.

"Are you certain you are all right?" Gillian asked the moment the door closed, and they found themselves again alone. "Because I know you've always been proud and—"

Growling, Colin grabbed his chair and turned it right side over. "You did not hurt me."

She'd done any number of things where he was concerned this day:

She'd shocked him—several times.

She'd scandalized him.

Annoyed him.

She'd not, however, hurt him. At least not intentionally. That right had belonged exclusively to her father, the marquess.

She eyed him a long while before reclaiming her seat. "If you say so," she finally said, those four words, along with her knowing tone, indicating she thought him a liar.

This time, Colin folded his arms and remained standing. This exchange had already gone on for twelve minutes longer than it should have. "Gillian, I don't know why you want or need a husband—"

"Oh, you misunderstood me," she cut him off. "I don't want you to marry me."

"You don't," he stated.

She shook her head. "Of course not."

Of course not, she said. She just came in here with a child's contract and a lengthy statement about the terms they'd struck. And just like that, she'd turned him on his head again. He scrubbed a hand at his forehead, hoping to rub some clarity into any of this.

Gillian took mercy on him in his befuddled state. "I just need a betrothed until—" She abruptly silenced herself; going tight-lipped.

As a detective, Colin had learned to dissect every aspect of a person's words and actions, breaking each down into specific parts of a larger puzzle that could be solved as those pieces were revealed.

She *needed* a betrothed. Not *wanted*.

There was a distinct difference that raised all manner of questions. None of which, however, again, were his business. Her reasons for coming here to try to secure a fake betrothal from him were neither here nor there. It didn't matter, and he'd no inclination or interest in "helping" her. Yet, he found himself... curious anyway.

"Until?" That was, of course, the detective in him, the one who always craved obscure details so he could put them together and solve the puzzle.

Gillian shifted on the chair, the wood groaning under that slight movement. She stopped and held his gaze. "Just... until."

"You come here, asking me for marriage, which then becomes a fake betrothal, and think to do so without offering your reasons?"

She nodded slowly. "Yes, I think you have all of it."

And then it all made sense.

A sharp bark of laughter burst from him, and Gillian jolted under that expression of his wry mirth. And then she was joining in. Her shoulders and delightfully rounded frame shook with her amusement.

Of course. How had he not realized it before? "You're joking." She'd always had a stingingly clever, if peculiar, wit.

She stopped laughing, wearing the same affronted expression she had when he'd called her mad.

His laughter faded. "You're not."

She shook her head.

Colin consulted the timepiece on his desk. This had really gone on long enough. The longer she was here, the greater the chance of scandal. As it was, his clerk knew she was here, and though he didn't doubt the young man's loyalty, no good could come from a Farendale being here.

"Gillian, do you know what I've been doing these past years?" he asked bluntly.

She nodded, briefly shocking him with that revelation. "Of course I do." Gillian gave him a pointed look. "That is, after all, what friends do. They keep contact. And if they do not, then they stay abreast of the other's life."

Unlike him.

In fairness, his and his mother's future had been dependent upon him cutting all ties with the marquess's daughter. The past, and the end of their childhood friendship, was not something he had the time or inclination to get into. The past was called "the past" because that was precisely where it belonged, and the only relevance it played was in cases he was solving. And the present and future didn't allow a bastard-born detective to call a marquess's daughter *friend*. He'd opened his mouth to gently show her the door when she spoke.

"You've done very well for yourself," Gillian said softly, moving her gaze around his office.

Discomfited by that praise, he shifted his weight from side to side. "I investigate murders and thefts. I help men who are being bribed or who've been swindled," he went on, shifting the conversation away from her praise. "Every minute of every hour of every day is filled with my work." And this meeting had gone on longer than it should have. "I don't know your reasons for coming here, but I don't have the time to play at whatever games you are playing." This time.

Those days had ended long, long ago, when he'd been thrown off her family's properties.

Gillian's lower lip trembled, the flesh quivering so very slightly that had he not been studying her face as close as he had, Colin would have missed it. Her teeth closed over it as she brought that tremble under control. "I… see." She came to her feet. "I wish you continued success in your work, Colin." Drawing her hood over her head, Gillian headed for the door.

He studied her as she retreated. Her back was proudly erect, her shoulders back. She'd always been a queen in every exchange.

"Gillian?" he called out when her fingers landed on the handle.

She stopped, facing him once more. That deep muslin hood kept her expression a mystery.

"Are you in some kind of trouble, Gillian?"

She laughed. "That is your detective mind at work, imagining great troubles everywhere."

Only, that laugh… It hadn't been the full, husky one that had always ended on a snort, marking that laugh as the lie it was. With that, she left.

Finally.

Now he could return to his work.

Colin grabbed for the list of potential cases his clerk had presented him with. While he scanned the information there, he tapped the edge of his desk in time to his ticking clock.

That is your detective mind at work, imagining great troubles everywhere.

Unbidden, his gaze drifted up and over to the doorway Gillian had exited through a short while ago.

She'd been lying. That much was clear.

Over the years, he'd developed an ability to compartmentalize any and all feelings. Pity and sympathy were dangerous emotions that had no place in a detective's existence—that was, not any good detective's.

Gillian Farendale, however, was the daughter of the marquess who'd ordered Colin and his mother off his property. The ruthless, career-minded person he was should focus on nothing more than that.

And yet…

Colin's fingertips ceased their tapping.

Opening his center desk drawer, he fished about—and found—an old sheet of vellum. Colin tugged it out and read through several times the words written there.

What in hell was he thinking?

With a curse, he shoved it to the bottom of the stack of papers.

Bold, proud, and courageous, as she'd ever been, she wasn't a woman who'd ever want to elicit the sentiments of pity and sympathy in anyone. But she'd come to him… looking for help. Even as she'd not explicitly asked for it.

When he'd asked if she was in trouble, she'd not denied it.

What could be so dire as to send a young lady fleeing to a detective she'd known long ago to put such a request to him?

Giving up on the pretense that he could focus on something other than his peculiar afternoon visit, Colin shoved aside the potential cases.

She'd not asked to enlist his services. Rather, she'd wished for a pretend husband.

Or, as she'd clarified, a pretend *betrothed*.

She wasn't in need of help that was permanent. Otherwise, she'd have held him to the full terms of that child's contract.

Trouble.

There could be no disputing the fact that her trouble was something significant enough, dire enough that she'd chosen to seek the help of a stranger.

And, as nonsensical as her ask of him had been, he knew only one certainty: He needed to get to the bottom of whatever threat she faced.

CHAPTER 5

¶IF ONE WERE TO FLAUNT a fake betrothed to one's parents in order to circumvent an unwanted betrothal, one had better have a fake betrothed.

Having returned, decidedly betrothed-less, Gillian found herself summoned for a second round of parental displeasure.

"You are a disgrace. A horrible, filthy, shameful disgrace."

As her father towered over her, she remained motionless in her seat, her gaze forward. Had she respected her father, his acerbic words would have likely hurt a good deal more than they did. As it was, through his tirade, she was able to think of just one thing: Colin.

Are you in some kind of trouble, Gillian?

Standing as close as she'd been to him in his office, she'd known intuitively that had she said *yes*, he would have offered his help. Oh, mayhap not to the terms she'd asked of him. But she'd not wanted his assistance.

Not like that.

Not by being the pathetic, piteous, desperate creature who'd sought him out after years and years of not having seen each other.

Because she still had her pride.

Nay, it wasn't just a matter of pride… it was a matter of self-preservation, too.

Now, however, seated in her father's offices, she rather wished she'd at least considered putting her pride aside.

"You are taking this a good deal better than I thought you would," she murmured. It was a lie. He was taking this about as well as she'd anticipated.

There were several beats of long, dangerous silence. Her father's eyes bulged in his face. He thundered incoherent rage.

Incoherent and unable to get out proper insults? Nay, he was taking this even worse than she'd anticipated.

From the seat she occupied beside Gillian, her mother wept into a balled-up kerchief. "Shh," the marchioness pleaded with her husband. "Anyone might hear."

Her father turned his dark rage on his wife. "You've ordered all servants from this corridor. Am I to trust that you've failed as a wife in this, too?"

Color splotched her mother's cheeks. "I-I am not a f-failure. I cannot be held accountable for... for... this," she said on an indignant huff.

Yes, because ultimately, what had always mattered more than either of her own disappointing daughters was how those disappointing daughters reflected upon her, the all-powerful, much-*respected*, and, more, feared marchioness.

"You would think to wash your hands of this? First, there was Genevieve."

The marchioness sputtered. "You should blame me for Genevieve?"

Yes, that was of course what her and Genevieve's devoted mother should focus on—being held to blame for her daughter's failings.

"And why should I not? You are their mother. The one responsible for seeing they were properly instructed on propriety."

"'Properly instructed on propriety,'" Gillian silently mouthed as her parents continued their quarreling. A memory slipped in of herself as a young lady standing before a mirror, a stern governess behind her, forcing Gillian to complete those drills.

Peter Piper picked a peck of pickled peppers;
A peck of pickled peppers Peter Piper picked;
If Peter Piper picked a peck of pickled peppers,
Where's the peck of pickled peppers Peter Piper picked?

How many times had she been forced to endure ridiculous elocution lesson after ridiculous elocution lesson based on John Harris' *Peter Piper's Practical Principles of Plain and Perfect Pronunciation*? How much of her life had been wasted as her parents had tried to stuff her into those constraints expected of ladies? And still tried, even as she was a woman of twenty-four years of age.

"With Genevieve as her sister, there was no hope or help for her. The blame belongs squarely with her," her mother was saying.

Oh, this was really quite enough. Genevieve was an accomplished artist. She was a loving mother and loyal friend. None of that, however, would matter to the marquess and marchioness. Either way, she'd be damned if they dragged her sister's name because of Gillian's sins.

"Genevieve is a marchioness and will one day go on to be a duchess," she said coolly. "By your terms of what is important, I think she should be raised up by you and lauded for her marriage."

Two sets of rage-filled eyes swiveled to her.

For a brief moment, she wished she'd kept silent and let them continue to tear each other apart. She slipped lower into the folds of the winged chair she occupied.

"Your *sister* married a wicked rake."

"He's reformed," she felt inclined to point out, defending the brother-in-law who'd become endlessly devoted and loving of his wife and their two children.

"And that rake is the one responsible for putting romantic thoughts into her head," the marchioness snapped. "Certainly not me."

And Gillian was saved as her mother, devoted to her title as leading hostess, redirected her anger back to her husband's earlier criticism of her own *accomplishments*. "You were the one who allowed her to marry that scoundrel. I was the one who insisted she marry Lord Tremaine."

Father slammed his fist down in the middle of his desk, and the ledgers there jumped. "That is *rubbish*. Utter rubbish," he bellowed. "You are misremembering and rewriting what happened."

It was vastly easier for them to debate Genevieve's blissfully happy union than Gillian's current circumstances.

"Am I?" Mother winged an icy brow. "You saw the possibility of being connected to a dukedom." Mother shuddered. "If I'd had my way, Genevieve would have never wed a rake and Gillian would have never had the idea to attend such an affair and behave as she did."

Resentment had a taste and it was biting like vinegar. Behave as she did... Because that was how her mother and father and the whole world would view what transpired that night: it was all Gillian's fault.

And they aren't wrong, are they? a voice taunted.

"Well, girl?" Father snapped. "Do you have nothing else to say?"

This was where she'd planned to toss her betrothed in their faces and save herself from whatever scheming inevitably followed whatever was about to come. She'd endured their disparagement, their disappointment and fury and rage. She always had.

Gillian made herself sit upright. "What is there to say?"

The fight seemed to go out of her father. He sat heavily in his chair, falling back into the folds. "What, indeed?" he muttered, wiping a hand over his face. "Who is he? The man you insist is your betrothed."

Her mind sputtered to a halt. She'd not anticipated... this. "I... would rather not say at this time."

Mother jumped to her feet and punctuated her words with a finger toward the sky. "Because there is no betrothed. I told you."

The marquess briefly closed his eyes. "Thank goodness for small measures. As I see it, there are two options."

She stiffened. This was the moment she'd ultimately feared. When they set about dictating and directing her fate.

"One, she can go to the properties left by your father."

Your father, as in Gillian's late grandfather. Her heart twisted as she thought of his recent loss. That wording also meant, however, that Gillian's father had shut her out of the discussion and was going about orchestrating her life, with the help of his wife.

"Or she can wed Lord Barber."

Absolutely not. Never. *Ever.*

She raised a hand. "I'll retire to the country until... until..." How long was a fallen lady banished to the country for? Were there even standards for these sorts of things?

Mother nodded. "I agree."—well, this was certainly a first: Gillian and her mother having a like thought—"At which point, if there is a product of... of... whatever happened... it can be taken care of."

A product? What was her mother... "There is no babe," she said quickly. That had been the small miracle to come from this. Never had she been more relieved for her menses than she had been that day they'd commenced following that night with Lord Barber.

Her father coughed into his fist, his cheeks as red as the crimson stripe in the Union Jack flag.

"She'll marry Lord Barber," he said as if Gillian weren't there. As if they were not discussing her fate and future.

Gillian seethed. "I will *never*—"

Her father quelled her with a look. "I'm not asking you."

"Your options, given the circumstances, are... limited," her mother added.

And for the second time that day, Gillian found herself agreeing with the marchioness.

In her mind, she frantically ran through every last option she'd considered these past weeks. "I... can go to Genevieve's." Even as she said it, she recognized the selfishness. Selfishness fueled by desperation.

"Your sister, who is even now struggling to bring another babe into this world? Do you truly think she wants or needs you and your troubles about?" the marchioness asked, and the absolute lack of inflection made those words somehow more ruthless.

Gillian bit the inside of her cheek. No. Genevieve, who faced another complicated pregnancy, while also having to care for the two children she already had, certainly didn't need to contend with the problems Gillian had brought upon herself.

While her parents launched into another diatribe, she realized the truth.

She had no one to turn to.

CHAPTER 6

The nobility were a proud lot.

They took care to show mastery of their emotions and matters.

And, as a rule, they did not raise their voices. Their brows and monocles, yes. Voices, never.

That understanding of how the lords and ladies of Polite Society presented themselves was not a product of Colin's own half-blood connection to a duke.

Rather, it was an understanding that had come in his many years of work.

In the time he'd worked as a detective, many of his assignments had, in some way or another, involved dealing with the nobility, be they clients or somehow men and women linked to cases he'd been investigating.

It was why, having found his way inside the Marquess of Ellsworth's household, that he had the answer to the question he'd put to Gillian: She *was* in trouble. For it needn't take a detective to ascertain that the shouts he heard were directly connected to whatever had brought Gillian Farendale to his offices earlier that morn.

Keeping close to the ornately silk wallpaper as he went, he trained his ears on those elevated voices.

Colin found his way down the empty corridors, heading toward the volatile exchange between the marquess and marchioness.

To Hold a Lady's Secret

Despite the fact that he and Gillian had been friends as children, Colin had only a handful of interactions with them. All of those exchanges had entailed them berating Gillian for continuing to keep company with him.

Now, their shouts came intermittently, punctuated by a pause of silence, followed by further yelling, which guided him the remainder of the way to the room.

Opening the door directly across the hall, he let himself into the darkened parlor and strained his ears, trying to make out the unfolding fight.

"…a disgrace," Lord Ellsworth spat.

For the years of self-control and indifference he'd built to the world's opinion, he was unable to keep his hands from balling into fists. It had been years since he'd heard those hated, crisp, pompous tones. Ones that had once been directed at him and his late mother and now were turned on another.

There came the sound of noisy weeping. "…shameful is what…"

Even with that panel shut and the distance between Colin and the marquess and marchioness, those insults came sporadic in their clarity.

Until there came a lengthy period of quiet.

The door in the hall opened and then closed with a hard *thwack*. A moment later, rapid footfalls followed, one heavy, the other light.

"You must contact him," the marchioness was saying.

"Not a word," Lord Ellsworth snapped.

The marquess' and marchioness' voices faded altogether.

Colin remained fixed to his spot alongside the entryway of the parlor. The ring of silence hummed in the air until, a moment later, he heard the faint click of that same panel being opened once more.

"That went remarkably well." Gillian's mutterings reached him.

Slipping from the room, he followed her.

Colin covered her mouth from behind.

Gillian stiffened and then promptly fought him, thrashing her arms, bucking her body against his.

"Quiet," he whispered against her ear as he drew her back into the empty parlor he'd just quit.

She immediately stilled. Her chest rose hard and fast, her breath coming in rapid pants against his palm.

He felt the moment some of the tension eased from her body. "Can I count on your silence if I lower my arm?" he whispered against her ear.

Gillian gave an unsteady nod.

Colin released his hold on her.

"Colin," she whispered, hurriedly pushing the door shut.

He stopped the panel before it closed and eased it slowly so that the click when it did shut barely resonated in the quiet.

Colin turned the lock.

"What are you *doing* here?" she asked, her voice nearly soundless.

"Never tell me, this is surprise from the same woman who showed up at my offices without an escort?"

"That wasn't breaking and entering," she pointed out.

Fair enough.

Gillian glanced about. "Furthermore, how did you gain entry?"

"With my skills," he said matter-of-factly. "It is what I do."

"You, a detective, sneaks inside households?"

He grinned wryly. "I prefer to think of it as moving stealthily, if the situation calls for it."

"It's all the same, just worded differently."

"Yes." Yes, it was. And debating the point with Gillian Farendale proved as enjoyable as all the previous exchanges he'd had with her. Which brought him to the whole reason for searching her out, against all logic and reason. They had an unsettled debt between them. "I came because I have questions." Questions about her circumstances and the reason the marquess and marchioness had been haranguing her just moments ago.

"The time for questions was at our last meeting." She held his gaze. "When you were more concerned with rushing me off."

His neck heated. "I wasn't rushing—"

Gillian winged a golden brow up.

Very well. He'd been attempting to hurry her out. "You asked me to play at being your betrothed."

Her eyes brightened as she sprang forward on the balls of her feet. "You've changed your mind."

"Absolutely not." He'd already told her that the last thing he ever intended to do was to marry. His work was his wife. But that did not mean he couldn't help her if she was in trouble.

Her expression fell. She immediately masked her features. "Then I'm not really certain why you've gone through all the effort of invading my family's household."

Invading? Colin's frown deepened. "I came to determine what desperation compelled you to seek me out." And having overheard the volatility of the exchange between her and her father, he'd gathered the marquess was in some way linked.

Gillian tipped her chin up a notch. "I'd hardly call it desperation."

No, proud as she was, she wouldn't.

"Why are you here, Colin?"

"I already told you—"

"Because you have questions. Yes, yes. You said all that." Gillian gestured between them. "But why are you really here? A sense of guilt because, as a former friend, you feel somehow obligated?"

A flush climbed his neck all the way up to his cheeks, and he gave thanks for the cover of darkness that shielded that telling color.

Except…

Gillian drifted closer and stroked a fingertip boldly down the curve of his cheek. "I see by your blush that I am, in fact, correct."

The heat there deepened. "I don't blush."

She leaned up close, placing her lips near his ear. "That may have been true before." Her breath, with a hint of vanilla and some exotic scent he could not place, caressed his cheek, distracting from her whispered words. "But you are now."

He was… now… what?

He was distracted and confused… because of her nearness. A nearness that highlighted a very dangerous discovery. Involuntarily, his gaze slipped lower, to the cream-white flesh revealed just above the top of a modest, lace-trimmed bodice.

She'd grown up.

Colin swallowed several times. Or he *tried* to. His throat struggled with that basic, reflexive movement.

And suddenly, he had a new reason to add to the long list of many for why he should not have come here.

Colin hastily backed up several steps and opened his mouth in a bid to reclaim the direction of their exchange.

She wouldn't allow it.

"That is it, isn't it? After I left, you had a moment of guilt set in." She glided toward him, and he made himself stand there as she erased that much-needed distance he'd put between them. "Perhaps you thought about our friendship?"

He had.

Gillian came closer still. "Mayhap you thought about how I treated you in comparison to all those other nasty villagers?"

The woman could be a damned detective.

And he was left wondering why she'd sought him out. One as astute and direct as Gillian Farendale was hardly in need of anyone's help.

Gillian's mouth tightened, those fully formed lips making a lush moue that he despised himself for noticing.

"Well, I've news for you, Colin. I didn't become your friend long ago out of pity. I did it because I *liked* you. And I didn't treat you with kindness because I felt badly about how others treated you, but rather because it's how I would treat anyone. Now… I thank you for at least coming here this night, but you are absolved of guilt and free to go." With that, she spun and headed for the door.

Colin intercepted her as she clasped the handle, covering her fingers with his.

Gillian's body tensed.

An electric shock sizzled along his skin, and the air around him seemed to come alive.

He should release her hand, and yet, if he did so, she'd leave. That was the only reason he still held her.

Liar. He was a damned liar. The satiny softness of her skin was a siren's luring, pulling him in. Colin lightly stroked the pad of his thumb along the seam of her wrist. Her pulse beat an erratic rhythm to match his own.

The audible rasp of her breathing filled the room and his ears as he slid near enough that her back brushed his chest.

Danger. Everything about Gillian Farendale screamed that word into the void of the silence filled only by their breathing.

Colin guided her around so they faced each other. "Are you in trouble, Gillian?" he asked flatly.

Only, why did it feel that the greatest trouble that existed was this inexplicable effect she had on him?

☙

Having sought out Colin, she'd expected that he would of course have to understand something of her desperation and the need she had of him in her life.

She'd envisioned their exchange; it would have simply been an easy discourse between two old friends. In her mind, she'd seen him as they'd been in their youth, as the person who'd always been so easy to talk to.

What she'd not anticipated was the actual prospect of having to confess all to him.

She'd not allowed herself to think of...*this*.

Was she in trouble?

The immediate and accurate answer was, in fact: yes.

She was in all manner of trouble, in every worst way a woman could be.

But to tell him that? To tell Colin that curiosity and boredom had led her to attend a shameful affair. And as if that was not mortifying enough, that she'd then gone off alone with a rake?

There was nothing easy about having this discussion... with anyone.

"Gillian?" he prodded, once again guiding her chin up, his touch methodical, his tone matter-of-fact.

Moments ago, she'd believed him as unsettled by her nearness as she was by his.

Imaginings were all that had been. That reminder, however, also grounded her.

"My parents insist I marry," she finally said.

"And you disapprove of the gentleman?"

Disapprove of a man who laced drinks and trapped ladies in the hopes of replenishing the money he'd lost wagering? A panicky laugh built in her throat. "Yes, I disapprove."

"Then tell them that, Gillian. They cannot force you," he said impatiently.

Was it just desperation to be done with her that accounted for that naïveté on his part? Or, with the passage of time, had he somehow *forgotten* the manner of person her father was and would always be?

"That is an unexpected take from a hardened constable turned detective." One whose exploits she'd followed deep within the scandal pages. He frowned. Another man would have blustered and sputtered at that charge. Not Colin, who was as coolly in control as ever. "You know my father, Colin," she said quietly.

A muscle rippled along his jaw, the only indication that he'd heard her and every indication that he agreed with her.

"And they wouldn't be satisfied if you marry someone else?"

"Oh, I'm certain they would be." As long as he had a title, of course.

He looked questioningly back at her and slowly shook his head as if puzzling through a riddle. "But you don't wish to marry?"

Who would have her now, aside from a scoundrel or desperate lord like Lord Barber? Not with her virtue gone and her reputation ruined. As such, the honest and immediate answer was *no*. Nor, for that matter, did she wish to make a match born of desperation. *What other options are there?* a voice taunted.

She felt his stare probing her, and Gillian made herself answer with a question of her own. "Do you want to marry?"

"Fair point."

Gillian gave a little grunt. "Of course it is." After all, the expectation among all, Colin included, was that it was perfectly acceptable and understandable when a man expressed a contentedness with never marrying. The moment a woman was of a like opinion, however, the world eyed her like she were sprouting a second head.

But then, it was that free thinking that had gotten her into the predicament she now found herself in. She'd wanted a taste of the passion that all the rogues, scoundrels, and widows were free to enjoy. *Enjoy.*

There'd been little to recommend her interlude with Lord Barber. And with the problem she faced, there was even less to recommend it now.

"So you don't approve of the match."

"I just said as much," she snapped. When had he become so thick? And furthermore… "There is no match."

"The match he's attempting to maneuver you into," he corrected.

"Really, Colin. If I approved, do you truly think I would have come to you with this?" Gillian shook her head. "You really are surprisingly obtuse with your questioning."

He bristled. "I beg your pardon. A detective asks every question, even the one that seems most basic."

"Well, that one was beyond basic."

"Every question has a purpose, Gillian."

Every question has a purpose…

And something in that, in being reduced from "friend he wished to help" to "the case he needed to solve," sent a sliver of hurt running through her. "I don't wish to marry. I don't want—"

To be tied forever to a man so vile he robbed me of my virtue.

Regret, pain, and shame all twisted and twined together, forming a knot in her throat. She felt Colin's questioning stare. "I don't want to be a grown woman whose life is still directed by my father and mother," she said. "I want to have freedom of my decisions and my choices." And it was decidedly her choice and decision to not marry the man who'd violated her trust and virtue. She hugged her arms close to her middle. "And of my future," she whispered, those words more for her than for Colin or anybody else. "I wish to be the one to make the decision about my future." When, in a reckless night of folly, she'd let herself be stripped of her decisions and choices.

"Why should your father choose now to force you into a match?"

Colin's quietly spoken question brought her eyes open. Why, when she was twenty-four years of age, hardly on the shelf? It was the right question. An astute one that acknowledged there was something more driving her father.

This was the part she'd ultimately known she would have to divulge, had he offered to help her. But he hadn't, and as such, she needn't have to answer him.

She opened her mouth to say as much when footfalls sounded in the corridor.

Gillian and Colin went absolutely motionless.

"You needn't worry. My father never looks for me," she whispered. It was that absolute disinterest in his daughter's life that had allowed her to sneak off as she had.

Even with her assurances, Colin slapped a finger to his lips, urging her to silence.

And then, those heavy footsteps stopped... outside their door.

Oh, hell.

The person on the other side of the panel gripped the handle and pressed it, attempting to open the door. "Gillian?"

There was a question there.

Oh, double hell.

Gillian felt all the blood drain from her cheeks. "It appears to be the one time he is looking for me," she whispered.

"Gillian? Is that you?"

Her heart hammered.

Colin moved his lips close to her ear, and she fought to quell a small gasp at the sensitive place his skin brushed. "Answer him."

This must be his detective's tone, the one that had earned him the reputation for being ruthless and cutthroat in his craft. And she shivered for altogether different reasons. Words failed her.

Thankfully, Colin was there, steadying her, as he'd always done. "Tell him you don't want to talk."

"I don't want to talk," she called out. Out of the corner of her eye, she caught Colin's sleek steps that carried him away from her and over to the window. Her heart fell. "Where are you going?" she whispered.

Of course, he needed to leave, and yet... once he did, she would be lost.

"I'm not going anywhere," her father called, incorrectly taking that question as his own.

She whipped her head back toward the door. "W-we've both said everything that needed to be said." Collecting her hem, she raced across the parlor to where Colin had lowered himself out of the window. She ducked her head outside and found him on the ground below.

"You dare think you're the one who'll decide that anything is at an end?" her father demanded. "By God, open the door this instant." He jiggled the handle again, this time more forcefully.

"Take me with you," she whispered as Colin headed down the alley.

For a moment, she thought—expected—he'd keep walking.

"…you are no daughter of mine, and the sooner I wash my hands of you, the better off this entire family will be…" Her father's bellows grew to a frenzy.

Colin stopped. His quiet curses reached her ears, and then—

Her pulse leaped a beat.

He marched back over to the gaping window and looked up.

Colin glared at her. "Well?"

"Well?" she repeated dumbly as her father pounded away at the door.

"Are you coming or aren't you, Gillian?"

She cocked her head as the meaning of that question hit her. "You are taking me with you?" she whispered in patent disbelief.

"Unless you've changed your—"

Gillian scrambled onto the windowsill and lowered herself into Colin's waiting arms.

With her father's shouts trailing after her, she did what she should have done long, long ago.

She left.

CHAPTER 7

AFTER COLIN'S BROTHER VAIL HAD rescued him from a life on the streets, Colin had committed himself to living a morally right existence. And it was a vow he'd lived by, never stealing again.

Until now.

That vow had been shattered this night.

Good God, I kidnapped a lady.

Though, given Gillian had willingly fled with him, whether it constituted kidnapping remained to be seen.

The lady's willingness, however, wouldn't matter to Polite Society. Polite Society need only discover that Colin, a mere "mister," and a bastard at that, had absconded with her. After he'd first invaded a marquess' household. That would mark the official end of his reputation and business. And of everything he'd built.

One, however, would never guess by her constant prattling, which had met him the moment he'd put her in a hack, that theirs was anything but a social visit.

"I cannot thank you enough for taking me with you."

He'd taken her with him.

His gut clenched, and he quickened his strides.

"No doubt you are worrying that my father will send up a search."

He'd *taken* a marquess's daughter.

This was bad.

All of it.

"Would you stop talking?" he snapped as he led Gillian the remainder of the way to the back entrance of his modest residence—a townhouse he rented out on Bruton Street, close to his offices and far enough away from Polite Society.

She immediately went quiet, and he immediately felt again like the village bully.

Colin silently cursed. "Forgive me. I'm... trying to think," he said gruffly. It was the first time in his career that he'd ever explained himself... to anyone. He jammed his key into the locked door.

Her stricken silence proved short-lived. "And you need complete quiet to do so?" Gillian rubbed at her bare arms. "That is certainly different than how you used to be. You were—"

He gestured impatiently for her to enter. "Sit," he said the moment he closed the door behind him.

Gillian glanced around the kitchens before taking up a place at the small square oak table. A plate had been left out, along with a small pitcher and cup, as they always were. Ignoring the dish, he took the seat across from Gillian... and simply sat there in silence.

Think.

What in hell was he going to do? Nay, more specifically—what in hell was he going to do *with her*?

Take her back. That was the immediate and obvious answer. No doubt servants and constables were already combing London in search of the missing lady. As such, Colin couldn't personally see to the task of returning her. But he could send her on her way. Alone in a carriage...

"You are having regrets."

"I didn't say that," he said tightly. He had, however, been thinking it, and she'd seen as much. The knowing glimmer in her clever gaze confirmed that.

"Either way, I am grateful. I know it is... problematic having me here, Colin."

Yes. He'd be ruined, and she would be, too. And it would all be because of one moment of rash impulsivity. He, who prided himself on being clear-headed and unfazed by any and every emotion. A skill that was essential for the work he did.

Gillian looked down at the plate.

He pushed it over to her.

"No, thank you."

They both went silent, sitting opposite each other, matched in their motionless.

Or mayhap, things had changed. After all, he wasn't the young, powerless boy he'd been in Cheshire. Now, he had the backing and support of a brother who was a baron, and through Vail, connections to peers that would surely offer some protection from the marquess...

Or mayhap he simply sought to convince himself that he'd not destroyed his future in taking Gillian with him.

"You're still not quiet," she murmured.

He grabbed the cup his brother Gavin had set out, and poured himself a drink. "I'm thinking, Gillian."

About how fucked he was.

"Do you want me to leave?"

"Do you have somewhere else you might go this evening?" he asked hopefully. "I trust your sister is in London?" He knew little about the ways of the nobility, but what he did know was that nothing took those lofty lords and ladies away from *ton* events at the height of the Season.

"I cannot go there." She'd always been close with her sister. Granted, the other woman was several years older, but he wondered at the reason for Gillian's adamance now. "Not at this time," she said softly, fiddling with the edge of the plate between them.

Colin drummed his fingertips on the side of his cup. "Miserable husband?"

"No."

"Violent?"

Her brows shot up. "Absolutely not."

"A rake?"

There was a slight hesitation.

That was it, then.

"He's not a rake. Not anymore," she added.

He snorted and took a sip of his coffee.

Gillian frowned. "That is a rather cynical way to view the world."

"That is a realistic way to view *people*."

"I disagree," she said, sitting back in her chair.

"Tell me of Lord Langley." The man had been the most ruthless bully toward Colin when they were boys. "What became of him?"

"What does he have to do with—?"

"Has *he* changed in the years since we were children?"

The corners of her lush mouth dipped slightly, deepening her frown. "He's…" She wrinkled her nose and said something under her breath.

Colin cupped a hand around his ear. "What was that?"

"He's not at all the kindest," she repeated, more loudly this time and more clearly.

"So, unchanged, then?"

"Just because some have not changed does not mean other people can't," she said softly. "My sister's husband *was* a rake." She stared blankly down at the tray. Picking up a flaky piece of bread, she plucked at the corners distractedly. "He's one of the changed ones." Her words came out quietly, as if she spoke to herself. Something darkened in her eyes, stirring a shiver of ice along his spine.

Colin sat back and studied her. What accounted for that abrupt shift to such somberness?

"And?" he prodded in the gentler tones he adopted when trying to pull certain secrets from suspects while he interviewed them.

The bread slipped from her fingers. "And he's very much devoted and in love with my sister," she said, with a finality indicating she'd no intention of saying anything further.

Doubtful. Once a rake, always a rake. Whatever image the gentleman might now portray as a devoted husband, he would always be a scoundrel. That was the way of a person's character—they were either good… or bad. Alas, Gillian had always been too innocent to own that truth. That naïveté remained. "Well, who is he, then, this paragon of a reformed rake?"

"I didn't say he's a paragon."

She was avoiding answering.

Oh, this was… interesting. With everything else she'd confided this day, what grounds would she have to keep the identity of her nobleman brother-in-law secret from him? "Who is he?"

"Marquess of Sain—"

His eyes flared. "The Marquess of... St. *Albans?*" And he couldn't help it, he burst out laughing. He laughed until his sides hurt and tears leaked from his eyes. And when his mirth started to slow, his merriment redoubled. His... brother. Or one of his many *siblings*. The Duke of Ravenscourt's legitimate son and heir. Years ago, he'd heard the other man was as much a reprobate as their *father*. "D-does this make you and I brother and sister, then?"

"Of course not. Unless you mean through law? In which case..."

He clutched at his sides and fought to breathe through his hilarity.

"Oh. You're teasing. *Hmph. This* is when you choose to find your sense of humor," she muttered.

When he'd finished, he found Gillian with her arms folded at her chest. "Are you done?" she asked.

"Yes." Though there'd been something... quite... nice in releasing that unrestrained amusement. He couldn't in his mind pull forth one single time in the near or even distant future when he had. Not since he'd left Cheshire.

That proved sobering and recalled him to the moment and the fact that the daughter of the same man who'd booted Colin's family from their property was before him now.

The only place his—and her—focus should be was on getting her out of his household, undiscovered, and seeing her somewhere else.

Anywhere else.

Gillian came to her feet. "I thank you for allowing me to stay."

Puzzled, he stared up at her. "You think you're... *staying?*"

Her face fell. She was utterly stricken, as he'd seen only once before, back when they'd struck that damned contract that had brought her back into his life. "I'm not?"

I'm not?

Say it. Get the words out.

He'd a business that was failing. A partner who wished to move them to Birmingham. And a sister, whom he'd foisted off on their brother—her half-brother—to care for.

Mayhap it was the fact that he'd proven less loyal and less a friend through the years. Mayhap it was a moment of madness. "You can stay," he said tersely.

Such hope lit her full cheeks and brightened her eyes, and it was like a sharp kick to the chest, this discovery that Gillian had grown up… into the entrancing woman before him.

"The night," he quickly added when the earth resumed its normal course. "You can stay the night."

Still, her relief remained, tangible in her clear blue eyes. "Thank you, Colin."

When she made no attempt to leave, he shook his head. "Is there something you need?"

She cleared her throat. "If you wouldn't mind showing me to my rooms?"

Another laugh burst from him. "Your rooms? I don't have *rooms*, and I don't have an army of servants. I have one bedchamber and one all-purpose servant." Not even really a servant, but rather one of Colin's loyal half-brothers who insisted on helping him.

A pretty blush filled her cheeks. "Oh."

They stood there, both locked to the floor. So close that the differences time had marked between them rose before him. Five inches shorter than his own six feet, two inches, she now had to tip her head back to meet his eyes.

And yet, that wasn't the only way in which she'd changed. Unbidden, his gaze slipped lower to the swells of her breasts and lower still to the curves of her hips.

He swallowed hard, despising the discovery in this moment that he was very much his sire's son. For how else to account for this unwitting awareness of all of her?

Gillian's tongue darted out, testing him further, fueling wicked ponderings of and for that sliver of pink flesh.

He balled his fists hard.

I am my damned father, after all.

"Behind you."

Confusion clouded her eyes. Gillian turned her head slowly, looking back, and that slight movement accentuated the long, graceful column of her neck, which was kissed by a heart-shaped birthmark just—

Gillian returned her focus forward, and his face hot, Colin took a hasty step away. "Your rooms are behind you, Lady Gillian."

Hurt contorted her features, there and then gone. "Thank you," she said softly.

With that, she closed the distance to the place he slept each night, let herself in, and then closed the door quietly behind her. And then, only the sound of silence remained so that he could almost believe this entire interaction—from her earlier visit, to his breaking into her family's household and ultimately absconding to his apartments with the lady—had been imagined.

Except…

The quiet shuffle of footsteps as she moved about his chambers proved this was very much real.

All of it.

CHAPTER 8

HE'D GIVEN HER A NIGHT.

Which was a good deal more than she deserved.

She'd come to him with an impossible favor, asking him to intervene against her father, and for what?

Because they'd once been childhood friends?

Still wearing the same garments she'd arrived in, Gillian burrowed deep into the feather mattress, and drew the quilted coverlet to her chin. She peered up at the canopy overhead.

From out in the other room, there came the faint but distinguishable clicking of a pen striking the surface of the table as Colin wrote. There was something calming in that rhythmic tap. And for the first time since she'd seen Lord Barber's carriage arrive at her home, some of the tension in her chest dissipated.

Gillian abandoned the attempt she'd been making at finding sleep, and sitting up, she scooted so that her back rested against the headboard.

Reaching for Colin's pillow, she drew it close to her chest and hugged it to herself.

Gillian had often thought of the first time she would make love.

As a young lady, she'd always secretly known there was something scandalous and wicked about her, because she had thoughts no woman should have. The more years that had passed and the more she'd observed the actions of Polite Society and read about them in the newspapers, she'd noticed that more often than not the scandalous escapades of the nobility were lauded.

When gentlemen dallied, they were deemed rakes and earned interest from polite and impolite company.

Whereas ladies were expected to behave only a certain way and think only certain things. None of which allowed a woman free thought over wonderings about passion.

And she'd begun to ask questions about the unfairness of those differing standards.

The more she'd thought on it, the more she'd railed at the unfairness, and she'd begun to let herself to her wonderings, without guilt. So she'd imagined what it would be like to taste passion. In all those wonderings, there had always been a bed. And there had been magic and excitement and delicious shivers as she lost the ability to do anything but feel.

The reality had been far different than those romantic imaginings found in the pages of Gothic novels and scandalous poems.

There'd been no glorious sensations. Why, for her, there weren't even memories of what had come that night.

Tears burned her eyes, and she angrily brushed them away.

There'd not even been a bed. Shifting in the deep, soft mattress that Colin had sacrificed for her, she allowed herself to her regrets. And there were so many of them.

When she'd awakened the following morning, with an aching head, in an empty parlor, and to the horror of what had happened while she'd slept, she'd learned that her first time hadn't been in a bed… but on a sofa. A Chippendale piece with pale white fabric that had borne the remnants of what had transpired.

This time, another tear fell. Followed by another, and another, and she let herself to them.

Because that was what happened when one waltzed outside the edge of propriety with a scoundrel. It wasn't romantic, as books made it out to be. It wasn't magical and thrilling. It was just mistakes and regrets and callous men and regretful women.

And then there were men… like Colin.

Staring over the top of his silk-covered pillow, Gillian focused on that ornate panel overhead.

He'd called her out for making more of his residence than he felt there was. And yet, his bed was more comfortable than any she'd ever slept in. It spoke of just how well Colin had done for himself these past years. He'd begun a new life that he'd built with his own skill and strength.

Colin, who'd always been honorable, who'd secreted her away when her father had come for her, stuffed her into a nearby hackney, and ordered the driver onward to his residence. Even as his actions put him and his focus on his career at risk. And where desperation had driven every thought and action before this, in the quiet of his modest chambers, she owned all the reasons it was wrong of her to be here. None of which had anything to do with her or her reputation. Her reputation was already beyond ruin. For when she rejected Lord Barber—which she would—he'd sing tales of her sins for anyone who would listen.

And everyone would.

And they'd do so gleefully, because that was all Society cared about.

They didn't care about young ladies who'd been wronged or what those same ladies wanted for themselves in life.

No, to the whole world, the young woman was to blame for whatever ill befell her, and that included the heinous violations carried out by the likes of Lord Barber.

Just as Society wouldn't ever dare take the side of a man of illegitimate birth who'd built an entire life for himself.

Even if Colin Lockhart was more honorable than all the lords in London combined.

It had been wrong to seek out Colin. She had asked him for an untenable favor without any true consideration of how her scandal would be eventually found out, and when it was, those linked to her would be dragged down into the mire of gossip and ill opinion that awaited.

"He deserves better than that," she whispered.

Drawing in a shuddery breath, she swung her legs over the side of the bed, heading for the washbasin.

At some point before their arrival, the one servant Colin had spoken of had set out a basin of water and shaving supplies.

Tentatively, she picked up a blade and studied the fine article.

She'd imagined this, having a relationship so intimate as to know the manner of blade her husband preferred and used.

She made herself put the blade down, beside the brush that rested there, and looked at herself in the mirror.

Red, swollen eyes and puffy cheeks stared back from the beveled glass. Grimacing, she leaned down and splashed water on her face.

The water was cool, and she welcomed the balm against her skin. When she'd finished, she collected his towel and patted her face.

Then, not allowing herself to procrastinate further, she headed back across the room.

Before her courage deserted her, Gillian let herself out and found him. His back was to her where he was seated at a desk… working.

Was he always working?

"You're out of bed," he noted, not bothering to look back.

Gillian hugged her arms to her middle. "You heard me."

"I hear everything," he said, in a statement that coming from another would have been arrogance, but from this man came as matter-of-fact, inspiring confidence for it.

Her gut clenched. What else had he heard? Her crying? Mortification gripped her.

After all, pride might not be much, but it was all she had left.

"I take it you find your accommodations less than what you're accustomed to."

She frowned. Was that why he believed she'd come out here? "No," she said softly. "I have no complaints. They are perfect."

Colin snorted.

How very low his opinion was of her all these years later. Or was it a reflection of his opinion on his own accomplishments and things? Or… was it a combination of the two?

Hovering at the doorway, Gillian waited for an invitation to join him… that did not come.

She let her arms fall to her sides. "What are you working on?" she asked, stalling, knowing she needed to confide in him and be gone, but still not knowing how or where to start.

"I'm considering cases." There came a rustle as he turned the page in his book.

How different he was from all the lords of London. A self-made man, he'd risen up to create a life for himself. He wasn't one to live for his own pleasures and scandalous pursuits.

And what have I truly done? What of any real importance, that was?

Her greatest attempt at having some control of her existence had left her hopelessly *without* control.

Gillian moved closer, stopping at his shoulder, and when he extended no offer, she took it upon herself. Clasping the back of a chair, she sat in the seat closest to his.

He stiffened, but didn't pick up his head. A dark curl hung over his brow, and her fingers ached to push the strand back. Forcing her gaze away from those tempting curls and over to the stacks of pages that so occupied him, she found herself with a new—and different—fascination where Colin Lockhart was concerned.

"How do you decide?" she asked curiously.

He frowned.

For a moment, she expected he'd tell her to mind her own business and deny her an answer to a question she had no right to.

"I look at the case presented," he said gruffly. "I look at the complexity. And then I determine if I'm the person best able to solve it." Colin's broad shoulders moved up in a little shrug. "And then I do."

That was it. *And then I do.* The assuredness to his statement would inspire confidence in anyone.

Nor did it escape Gillian's notice that he didn't mention the funds to be earned. It wasn't about which client could pay him the most. Or bring the most prestige.

Rather, he spoke only about the case and whether he felt he was one to help solve it.

Once more, that reasoning set him apart from most anyone else and also heightened the sense of guilt that she'd come to him, when he had so many others reliant upon him. He was a man of honor. Not the manner of man who'd deceive ladies and slip something into their drinks.

"That is… amazing."

"I take the work that is there, Gillian."

Except... that wasn't what he'd said. Somehow she knew if she debated him on that point, he'd dig in. She knew it because she'd known him and could see that streak of pride ran deep in him still.

He resumed working.

He wanted her to go.

She knew it because she'd always known when he wanted to be rid of a person's company. This was, however, the first time he'd turned that on her.

It was understandable. He was a grown man with business to see to, and she was nothing more than a distraction. A reckless moment, prompted by her plea and her father's unexpected arrival, had led him to take her with him. They were no longer children. Why, by his distance and aloofness, they weren't even friends.

As such, she should go.

And yet, oddly, knowing all that to be true, she felt the same... comfort that had always come in being near Colin.

It was the height of selfishness for her not to grant Colin that which he wished—her absence—but she could not bring herself to go. Because when she did, the reality of her circumstances and her absolute lack of control over her life and Lord Barber's pursuit would return. And this time, when she returned home, there would be no escaping that which her parents required and what the viscount wanted and what she desperately had no wish to do—marry some reprobate to spare her reputation.

෴

She wasn't going to leave.

She'd not been deterred by his singular focus on his work, but rather had taken a chair and seated herself.

No, she'd quite settled in, moving her gaze over his home office the way she might study some exhibit at the Royal Museum.

And... she'd been crying. That detail had not escaped him either.

Before she'd left the bedchambers to join him at his desk, his writing had been interrupted by the sound of her tears. It had been faint and almost undistinguishable, but his ears had recognized that sound for what it was. And it'd hit him like a kick to the gut.

It was, simply put, an unexpected response for him. In his

work, he dealt with men and women of all ages and stations and circumstances who cried before him. Some showed real emotion. Most of it was affected. Others cried from fear. There were so many tears, he'd become immune to them.

Yes, he and Gillian had once been friends, but he'd not seen her in almost as many years as he'd known her. As such, he should have been largely unmoved by that evidence of her misery, if for no other reason than because he'd not believed himself capable of feeling anything when a person wept.

Only to find… he'd been wrong.

So he'd listened to Gillian, alone in his rooms, attempting to stifle the sounds of her tears. That pride had always been a part of her. Something he'd admired her for.

She'd grown from a proud young girl into a woman.

One who also came to you for help, a voice reminded him.

Sighing, Colin gave up on his attempts to work and to dissuade her from remaining. "You're unable to sleep?"

She nodded.

Gillian of old would have prattled on with all the reasons for her sleeplessness and then launched into a list of games they might play that would aid her.

"What happened?" he asked gruffly.

That seemed to immediately transform her back to her former self. "Oh, no, your bedchambers are truly fine. Your bed, one of the finest—nay, the finest I've ever slept in," she hurried to assure him, and he might almost believe whatever had driven her to sadness had since gone.

He'd be wise to let her to her erroneous opinion, that he'd been asking after her chambers and not about the source of her upset. The reason she'd fled her family's household and risked her reputation to come with him to his residence. It would be the wiser and easier course, the uncomplicated one that wouldn't drag him any further into whatever it was that Gillian dealt with.

But for reasons he could not understand, ones that mayhap had to do with their past history, he could not let it go. "I was asking about your father." With that coldhearted, ruthless marquess, who'd thought nothing of tossing out two children and an unwed mother, it could really be anything.

"Oh." Gillian pressed her fingertips together and flexed the digits, attending them as she did so as if they contained the answer to his question.

She didn't wish to answer, and that only fueled a greater need to know about what troubles she, the cherished daughter of a marquess, could possibly face. He also knew, from his work, that it wasn't best to press a person for information. No matter how long the wait, it was best to allow that individual to speak when, and if, they were ready.

At last, she stopped that distracting little movement with her fingers, resting them flat on the surface of his desk. "I attended a masquerade."

He frowned. "That hardly seems reason to send him into a rage." But then, he'd also gathered that things didn't always make sense where the nobility were concerned.

A bright red blush blossomed on her cheeks. "It wasn't just a masq…" She trailed off under her breath, looking about his office.

Colin continued to give her the time she needed.

She finally met his eyes. "It wasn't just a masquerade," she repeated. "It was a scandalous one."

"A scandalous one…?" The only affairs he attended were those where he sought information related to a case. Those invitations through the years all had been managed by his brother Vail, thanks to the title he'd earned fighting Boney's forces.

Her gaze dipped once more. "A wicked one. Outrageous things happen at them, Colin. Terrible." At his continued silence, she spoke on a rush. "People making love in the middle of the room, and trading partners, and drinking and… and… exposing themselves and—" That color deepened to a shade of red that threatened to set her face afire. Her lips pulled in a distasteful grimace, and she gave her head a shake.

Ah. Those manner of affairs. The ones rumored to be frequently attended and hosted by reprobates… like the duke who'd sired him.

"Curiosity or a rake?"

At her quizzical look, he added, "I take it you were there for one of those reasons?" He lifted a brow. "Unless it was another?"

She dropped an elbow onto the table and buried her cheek in it. "The former. It was the former."

A tension he'd not realized he'd been holding left him. Something in thinking of her lured by a charming rogue onto the path of the wickedness she spoke of had left a sharp, stinging taste in his mouth.

"It was an event my sister attended once, in search of her husband."

"Ah, the reformed one."

She nudged his arm with her shoulder. "That was before he was reformed."

"And so you wished to attend?"

"I did." Her voice was distant. Her gaze sad. "I've attended balls and soirees and dinner parties. Every day of my life is remarkably the same. I'm nearly twenty-five-years old, and I've never experienced anything remotely exciting." Her lips twisted in a bitterly painful smile. "And this was going to be that excitement."

She'd always taken charge of what she'd wanted, their friendship, despite her father's and mother's disapproval, having been just one. She'd not changed in that regard either. And seeing her, bereft and shamed by her father for having attended that masquerade, stirred an old familiar fury with the marquess.

"Gillian, there is nothing wrong with you having acted on your curiosity," he said gently. "There is a double standard that exists, and it's hardly fair to judge men differently than women for attending."

Her lips parted slightly, and her heart-shaped features softened. "I... I've never heard any gentleman speak so."

Unnerved by the adoring gaze that moved over his face, he shifted in his chair. "Yes, well, I'm not a gentleman, so there is that, perhaps, for an explanation."

Gillian leaned forward and covered his hand with her own. "You're more gentleman than any man with any title, Colin Lockhart." She spoke with an adamancy that bespoke the truth she felt in that declaration.

It was why he'd always cared about her. It was why he shouldn't have sent her away when she'd come to him all these years later, out of the blue, and in search of his help. And it was also why he'd made the decision to invade her family's household and seek her out.

His gaze slipped to those long fingers that rested on his. Her hand, delicate and soft and perfectly manicured, against his callused, ink-stained, and scarred one. Their palms alone told tales of the station differences between them.

Ones she'd never cared about.

She followed his focus downward to their joined palms, and misunderstanding the reason for his study of them, Gillian yanked her fingers back. "Forgive me."

Colin waved off her apology.

Gillian drew in a shaky breath. "Either way, Society isn't of the same enlightened opinion as you."

Bastard-born, always far beyond the sphere of respectability, he wouldn't be. He'd never understood that world she and his father, and now his half-brother, belonged to, and he'd no desire to.

She eyed his cup of coffee, and he pushed it gently toward her.

With a murmured word of thanks, Gillian picked it up and took a small sip. She grimaced slightly before setting the glass down. "I do know it was reckless, though. Curiosity doesn't forgive bad decisions."

Once again, that earlier unease simmered to the surface.

Coward that he was, he didn't want any more of this telling, but mayhap he wasn't the terrible friend she'd accused him of being, because he also needed her to share what she needed to share.

❦

Why was he being so… nice?

Because that was how he'd always been… to her.

Whatever awkwardness and tension distance in time had put between them had somehow come down.

Mayhap that was what allowed her to sit with him now and at last confide in someone that which had haunted her these four weeks now.

"You don't need forgiveness for having gone to that event, Gillian," he said quietly.

And damn the tears that pricked her lashes. He wouldn't feel the same when she shared all of the truth. Unable to meet his eyes, she took another sip of his awful drink, which didn't know whether it wished to be coffee or tea and had somehow settled for some horrid variation of the two.

"It is," he said.

Confused, she picked her head up and looked at him.

He nudged his chin at the glass she still held. "Tea and coffee mixed together. My brother's creation."

"Your brother? Lord…Chilton?" She'd stumbled upon Colin's connection to the baron in a gossip column. From that point on, she'd made it a point of searching for and finding any further mention of Colin.

Colin smiled. "No. Not Vail. I have another. Many others," he added wryly. "The one who helps me here, is named Gavin."

And there came a different sadness this day… at all she'd missed about Colin and his life.

"He previously oversaw my other brother Vail's household, but came to feel I required assistance, and has since taken on the role of second butler at Vail's, while spending his days here, helping. He's quite devoted, and knowing I have an equal preference for tea and coffee, he had the idea to blend the two together so I could have both."

"And do you like it?" she asked quizzically and made herself take another experimental sip to see if she were missing something in terms of taste. She grimaced, and when she looked across the rim of the glass, she found him smiling.

"I quite despise it. It is truly horrendous stuff, but Gavin takes pride in it." And he didn't wish to hurt the other man's feelings.

Her lips formed their first true smile that day.

"Here, let me help you," he volunteered, and taking the mixed brew, he proceeded to drink it in one long, quick swallow.

When he finished, Colin winked. That slight flutter of his lashes sent her heart into a hard beat.

"It eventually grows on you."

"Does it?" She arched her neck, peering across the desk and into the dubious contents of his cup.

"No," he lied, pulling a laugh from her.

And here, she'd thought she'd never laugh again. She'd thought there would only ever be a dark cloud of regret and misery and fear following her.

Her smile faded as she looked over at Colin.

She knew what he was doing. She knew he was trying to drive back her earlier sadness. And another part of her fell in love with him again for being a man who cared enough to do that.

"I convinced my friend Honoria to accompany me," she said quietly. As the last of her unwed friends, Honoria had been the perfect partner to take along. "She thought it was folly." And it had been. Everything would have been different had Gillian just listened. "She insisted it was silly. A mistake to go to such a place. We were separated for a bit."

A bit.

It was the best she could offer, as she'd no real recollection of time that night. They'd become separated when she'd willingly followed a dashing, masked rake. He'd handed her a flute of champagne, overly sweet and odd-tasting, and then…there'd been everything that had come after.

Eager to have it over with, she made herself say it. "I was ruined, Colin." She grimaced. Only that wasn't quite accurate. It wasn't accurate at all. She'd *let* herself be ruined.

At last, she made herself look at him. And she wished he hadn't. She wished she'd held on to the brief moment when his smile had been real and his words reminiscent of the past.

He stared blankly at her.

Oh, God. This was even worse than she'd anticipated. All ten of her toes curled up into the soles of her foot, and her arches cramped from that tautness. And because he still gave no outward reaction to her confession, she clarified further for him. "I… lost my virtue." A panicky little giggle climbed her throat. She'd lost her virtue. How utterly ridiculous that sounded. As though it was something that could again be found.

"Your…"

She waited for him to finish that echo.

When he didn't, she did so for him. "My virtue, Colin." When he still sat there blankly, she snapped, "My virginity. My innocence."

All of it.

His proud, square jaw tensed. But he said nothing.

Somehow, that silence was all the more damning and all the more painful for it.

"This is the reason for your parents' anger earlier."

His wasn't a question. In fairness, though, there were all manner of things they were angry with her over. "Partly. The gentleman responsible for my *education* that night has since come forward. That apparently was part of his plan. To slip something into my champagne, bed me, then wed me. For my dowry, of course." Silence fell once more. Gillian glanced down at her hands. "And I know what you are thinking." Just like her mother and father, Colin was no doubt of the opinion that Gillian should wed Lord Barber.

"And what is that?" he asked in a quiet tone.

"That I should wed him. That I invited my own trouble that night, and therefore, I should have to pay the consequences." Gillian came to her feet. All the while, she avoided his eyes, not wanting to see the disgust there. "I thank you for coming to my household tonight and for taking me with you." And listening. Regardless of how he might now feel about her and the decisions she'd made, there'd been something cathartic in sharing her mistakes of that night… and regret. She lingered a moment, staring down at the glass his brother had prepared for him. "I'm so very sorry that I've invited potential trouble into your life." Gillian started for her rooms. *His* room. As she walked, she felt his gaze on her, following her.

"Gillian?"

She stopped and made herself turn back to face him.

Colin stood, and moving out from behind his desk, he took several steps toward her and then stopped. "You are wrong."

Her stomach clenched.

"I don't think you should wed him. I don't think that, at all." Fury burned to life in his eyes, hot and piercing from the intensity of it. "I do, however, think I should kill him."

A memory from long ago came back to her. Their first meeting, when she'd been bullied by Lord Deverly and had climbed a tree…

only to find Colin there.

"Oh, hello."

Nudging his chin, the little boy motioned toward the ground. "Do you want me to kill him for you?" he whispered.

Gillian considered the boy darting about the copse, searching everywhere for her. "No, I rather think I should like the honors."

He grinned.

"I'm Gillian."

"Colin."

Now, leaning up, she pressed a kiss to the small scar on his cheek that he'd earned when she'd been chasing him through the brook. "Thank you, but I'd see to the honors myself."

Gillian started for the door again.

"Gillian?" he called after her.

She cast a glance back.

His penetrating gaze held hers. "I wasn't jesting," he said quietly, and a tenderness offset the ice glinting in those emerald eyes.

She caught the inside of her lower lip. "Thank you." Not for the offer to hurt Lord Barber, but for having not passed judgment when anyone else would have. However, she'd never have him risk his reputation.

But isn't that what you did in going to him in the first place?

That was why she needed to leave. Sooner rather than later.

CHAPTER 9

OVER THE YEARS, COLIN HAD developed an extraordinary ability to listen when people spoke and separate his feelings from whatever details they shared.

He'd been a master, really, of remaining wholly unmoved, no matter what story was laid before him.

Separating his emotions was the only way in which to work on an assignment, because of the much-needed clear-headedness.

He'd been a master of it... until tonight.

Some rake had taken advantage of Gillian. He'd tricked her in an ultimate plan to trap her. Which was undoubtedly how many unions were formed.

And yet, this was Gillian.

And everything he'd told himself—that time had erected a distance between them, that they were both entirely different people, that he was unaffected by her presence and her story—had proven false.

An hour after her telling, he'd left her sleeping, and rage still burned his mouth, a vitriolic poison that pumped through his veins and carried with it the hungering to kill.

Gillian, defender of those who'd needed it—societal outcasts such as Colin had been, along with others in their quiet village—now found herself bullied... and threatened in the worst possible way.

"Well, given I never see you anymore, you are remarkably quiet, particularly for arriving here in the dead of night, needing to see me."

Catriona stood at the floor-to-ceiling-length window that overlooked the Mayfair streets below, her amused expression reflected in the glass.

A guilty flush climbing his cheeks, Colin faced his sister. "Forgive me." He consulted the mantel clock across the parlor. "Though it's hardly the dead of night."

Catriona snorted. "And that is hardly an apology."

Not for the first time that day, guilt sluiced through him. This was what he'd done, this was what he'd forsaken, becoming just like his father.

A mischievous twinkle lit her eyes. "I'm teasing, Colin," she said chidingly as she came over to join him. "I'm not in search of any apology, and you have no reason to give one. I know you are very busy."

He winced.

She swatted his arm. "Do stop it. I am not intentionally trying to make you feel guilty."

She needn't try. Guilt was always there. And had been since the moment his selfish friendship with Gillian had gotten Colin's sister and late mother forced out of Cheshire, and he'd had to resort to picking pockets just to keep them in a run-down apartment.

Catriona motioned to a sofa. "Sit. Sit. And tell me everything you've been up to."

He opened his mouth.

"Work," she supplied for him, that teasing glimmer back in her gaze. "I am teasing once more. For there is no doubt that is the only thing you've been up to, dear brother."

His lips quirked up at the corners. Any other time, that would have been an accurate supposition about what he'd been up to, because there was only one way he spent his days—working.

Catriona blinked several times and leaned forward, the satin of her skirts rustling. "Are you... *smiling?*"

He grunted. "I smile."

"No," she said, not missing a beat. "You do that"—Catriona

waved a hand in his general direction—"grunting noise of yours. You're very severe, you know."

He always had been. When he'd been younger, Gillian Farendale had been the only one to ever crack his guard and make him feel something other than the bitterness that came from his station as bastard-born son to a duke who'd no interest in him.

"And how is Mr. O'Toole?"

Insistent on moving them. The task he'd been charged with whispered at the back of his mind. To visit Birmingham and the potential investor in a Birmingham constable line. "He is as miserable as ever," he muttered.

"He at least smiles."

His frown deepened.

Catriona burst out laughing, and stretching a foot out, she kicked him in the shin. "I'm teasing you again." Except... her smile fell. "What is it?"

"It has been a long time since I have seen you."

"And?"

"And?" he echoed.

"Yes, well, it is just that it is ten o'clock."

"You were sleeping?" He made to rise.

She waved him back to his chair. "Of course not. It is... just that you are very predictable, you know. When you do visit, it is generally Sunday, and because most businesses are not open, and your workload is less."

It was another stinging testament to how single-minded his focus had become. How could he explain that Gillian's arrival had served as an unwitting reminder that he'd neglected his responsibilities as a brother?

"Are you happy here?" he asked suddenly.

"Am I...?" Catriona's brow puzzled. "That is why you came at ten o'clock at night?"

"With Vail and Bridget," he clarified. And more important... "They intend for you to join Polite Society soon." That had always been Vail's hope and expectation. Vail, who'd been made a baron and built an honorable life for himself and who was also immune to the same worries that dogged Colin at the idea of sending

Catriona out into the London wild.

Catriona reclined in her seat. "And?" she prodded, that twinkle back in her eyes.

"And..." She was going to be torn apart by the gossips. He made himself stop talking, to assemble his thoughts. She'd be hurt, and it would be because he again let it happen.

By the dawning light in her eyes, she'd realized the reason for his question. "And you believe it will be difficult for me entering the *ton*."

Yes. That was the immediate and accurate answer. The nobility had very specific rules as to who was permitted within their ranks. Catriona, however, saw Vail's success in that world and failed to see the *ton* for what it was.

And because one of them had hurt Gillian, then Catriona would only be like prey for some cad. The muscles of his chest seized painfully. "I'm here to see if this is truly what you want."

"Are you offering to take me with you?"

I don't want to go to him, Colin. You might know him, and he might be perfectly kind as you say, but he is a stranger. Take me with you.

"I can't do that," he said gruffly.

"I know, and this time, Colin, I'm not asking you to."

There should be only relief in knowing she'd found a home in Vail and Bridget's household, but there was also a failed sense of what he'd not been able to provide over the years. That which Vail had. As he had with all their half siblings he'd managed to locate, Vail had helped Catriona in ways Colin hadn't, or wouldn't have, ever been able to. Colin, who'd gotten them tossed from their family cottage and left them dependent upon his thieving to survive in the seediest end of London. No, honorable brothers didn't pass the responsibility of caring for one's sister over to another.

And what of Gillian Farendale? Who was there to help her? It was a question he'd not put to her that night, or at any point since she'd arrived at his office.

He glanced briefly down.

Catriona quit her King Louis armchair and joined him on the sofa. "You have always been the best brother."

The best brothers didn't get their sisters tossed from—

"I'm not saying this to hurt you," she went on, "but I do very much enjoy being here with Bridget and their babe."

Colin tugged one of her ringlets. "I'm not such a miserable brother that I wouldn't want to see you anything but happy wherever you are." He just knew from all of his dealings with High Society that the peerage would not provide her with happiness.

"You are worried about me being hurt," she murmured, revealing an intuitiveness that marked her very much his sister. "You are afraid I'll be rejected."

"You will be," he said, dispensing with subtlety, having learned the direct truth was far more important in protecting a person than giving them false assurances meant to assuage fears.

"Perhaps I will," she allowed. She lifted her shoulders. "But I am at peace with who I am and will embrace whatever experiences I am permitted."

In that, she proved braver than he.

"Now, enough of me. What of your business?"

Failing.

His business was failing. A combination of pride and shame prevented him from saying as much. He'd asked her to live with Vail while he'd set out to establish a firm to rival Bow Street. How to now confess that the venture was not only sinking, but that his partner was urging him to relocate outside of London?

He couldn't admit any of those failings. As such, through the remainder of their visit, he focused instead on details of the more interesting cases he'd worked—of which there were few. But she'd always enjoyed those tellings, and he was loath to disappoint.

"You know, you really should find more time for yourself, brother," his sister said as she walked with him to the front door. "Vail and Bridget miss you. And I miss you, and all our newfound family does, too."

Their newfound family—a small army of half siblings who'd all been wronged by the Duke of Ravenscourt.

Going up on tiptoe, Catriona kissed his cheek. "I really do believe you'd enjoy more this side of the world, if you just joined it."

He grunted. "I've—"

"Work," she supplied for him. "I know." This time, in place of the previous twinkle, there was a glimmer of sadness.

Sadness?

As she scurried off, Colin let himself out and headed for the boy holding the reins of his mount.

Catriona was too innocent to understand that she needn't pity him. He enjoyed the work he did. The decision to devote himself fully to it had been an intentional one. Where he'd had little to no control of his fate since he'd been a boy in Cheshire, he'd at last found something he was successful at. Something that had brought respect to his name and honor to his reputation.

But at what expense?

Climbing astride his stallion, Beau, he kicked the enormous creature onward to his residence.

He'd not given much thought—really, *any* thought—to anything other than his work. He was focused and dedicated, and in that, he'd neglected his sister. Whether she was cared about or for was neither here nor there. Catriona had been his responsibility. And yet, for all the ways he'd ceded his responsibilities, there'd been others to take on the mantle—those, as his sister had called them, found family.

What of Gillian Farendale? If he sent her back to her bastard of a father, what other family was there to help her? The sister who'd married an unreliable rake?

Or, you can provide her the help she sought.

His knees clenched reflexively, and Beau took off at a frenzied pace.

Cursing, Colin brought his mount under control.

Provide Gillian with help? That would require him to perpetuate a false betrothal. And when they broke it off, his reputation would be in tatters.

Unless, she was the one to break up with him. In which case...

"Stop," he muttered as he reached his residence. And yet, he couldn't. In his mind's eye, she was there, next to him at his desk, sharing the secrets of that night as if time hadn't been a distance between them and they were close friends still.

After he'd removed Beau's tack and brushed him down, Colin drew the stable door shut. As the wood gate slid into place, he looked at his mount, who stared accusingly at him.

"I don't owe her anything," he said tightly.

Beau whinnied and tossed his head.

His friendship to the lady had gotten him and his family tossed from Cheshire. That wasn't, and hadn't ever been, Gillian's fault. Colin had continued to ignore those directives from the marquess, because he'd selfishly been unable and unwilling to give up her friendship. "Fine," he amended. "But I don't owe her... I don't owe her... *that.*"

The stallion stamped his hoof several times in apparent equine disapproval.

Clenching the railing, Colin stared at the creature—the *loyal* creature. Loyal when Colin had proven far less so, where not only his sister was concerned, but with Gillian, too.

I swear, if you go near him, Barnaby Barnes, I will wallop you so good. And furthermore, what manner of boy with a name like Barnaby Barnes dares to go about bullying other children?

The memory brought his lips up in a wistful smile.

Beau nudged the hand Colin had rested on the slats.

Colin cursed. "Must you always be right?" he muttered into the quiet.

Beau stuck his enormous brown nose through the slats, and Colin softened that rebuke with a light scratch between the eyes. "Fine. You win. I'll help her."

Quitting the mews, Colin made the short walk to his townhouse. He let himself into the darkened rooms and pushed the door shut quietly behind him. Removing his cloak, he hung it along the stand beside the door. It was late. She was no doubt sleeping.

Sleeping in my rooms.

And he proved himself a bastard in every sense of the word by imagining her curled in his bed.

Giving his head a disgusted shake, he dislodged thoughts he had no place having. Not when she'd revealed everything she had about having been taken advantage of by some other cad. Colin headed over to the door of his bedchambers and lifted his hand to knock. He hesitated a moment, but then rapped lightly. "Gillian?" he called quietly.

Silence met his query.

Knocking again, this time with a more distinct thump, he called her name again.

Silence.

Unease tripped through him.

He gave another harder, more insistent knock.

Nothing.

Colin grabbed the handle and shoved the door open. His gaze did a sweep of the darkened room. The half moon that cast a bright glow through the open curtains illuminated, and emphasized, the empty bed.

Cursing, he did a quick inventory of the room and then, turning on his heel, searched the remainder of his modest townhouse. Already knowing, as he did, the truth.

He stopped in his office, that place where her chair sat precisely as she'd left it when she'd quit his side two hours earlier.

A slip of white paper propped against his crystal inkwell set stood out, stark in the dim light.

Striding over, he grabbed the folded page, flipped it open, and read.

I am sorry I put you in a difficult position. I thank you for the assistance you provided.

Your friend,

Gillian

His eyes remained locked on those two words. *Your friend.*

That was what she'd always been. Long before he'd known he had brothers, there'd been… her. It was why he'd owed it to her earlier that day to listen when she'd come to him for help. It was why he should have, if not agreed to the plan she'd proposed, at least concocted a different one to keep her safe.

And now… she was gone.

CHAPTER 10

GILLIAN HADN'T KNOWN WHAT SHE'D expected upon her return home.

No, actually she had.

She'd imagined histrionics from her mother. Further shouting and disparagement from her father. While thinking of what she was to face, she'd been more than half tempted to continue being selfish by remaining at Colin's. Where she was allowed to be… invisible. There'd been something so very free in that. In his townhouse, where there'd not even been servants underfoot, she'd been able to breathe.

But he hadn't promised her more than a day, and she'd been wrong to ask for even that.

So, when he'd left, she'd slipped out, too, and found her way by hired hackney back *home*, braced to meet the inevitable tumult.

In fairness, if she'd given it more thought, she would have realized that her parents were always a pair to resist emotional displays. To them, her return had somehow appeared to signal… defeat.

It was why, the following morn, they displayed no outward reaction to her return.

In fact, the following eve, as she sat on the carriage bench across from them on their way to Lord and Lady Grafton's ball, they so far had behaved as though that one outrageously unordinary day had never taken place.

But as their carriage rocked to a stop, her father glared at her. "Lord Barber informed me that he will be present," he said, speaking his first words to Gillian since she'd come back. "I assured him you aren't going to discourage his suit."

Her lips flattened into a hard line. "I'll not be ordered about." Not as he'd done with Genevieve. Gillian was ruined, but she'd no intention of selling her soul and the remainder of her days.

Her mother sputtered. "You dare speak to your—"

The marquess held up a hand, silencing his wife.

Her mother dipped her gaze to her lap.

Sitting there in silence, observing that domineering exchange, Gillian wondered whether there had been a time when her mother had ever had a voice. Had it been silenced by years of marriage to a soulless man who never saw her or treated her as an equal?

A man so different from Colin, who'd not passed judgment upon her. Who'd not held her to blame and who'd spoken to her as an equal.

Her father returned his attention Gillian's way. "Since you were a girl, you've persisted with your stubbornness. And you'd do the same now."

Was that what it was called when a woman refused to wed the cad who would take advantage of the woman he'd drugged? She bit the inside of her cheek hard to keep from saying as much. Nay, her father and mother would only ever see what happened as her fault.

"You have always been selfish," her father said.

A hiss exploded from between her clenched teeth. "You would call me selfish? You, who'd have me marry a fiend like Lord Barber?"

"Lord Barber, whose company you chose to keep that night," her mother piped in.

"Because of that, you'll have Genevieve's daughters pay the price, with their names being forever linked to their harlot aunt?"

At her father's words, she went absolutely motionless, that arrow landing squarely where the marquess had intended. For, in the ultimate twist of irony, her sister, who'd been so very worried about ruining Gillian's standing in Polite Society, should now find herself in that exact place.

A knock sounded at the carriage door.

A moment later, the driver opened the panel and handed down first her mother and then Gillian. She followed at a slower pace, her father's words haunting her through the long walk and interminable wait in the receiving line.

It was one thing for her name to be muddied and for her to own the consequences of her decision to go to that masquerade.

But for her nieces? Standing on the side of the ballroom dance floor, she stared vacantly out at the amorphous shapes as they twirled and whirled past in a dizzying blur.

When her sister had been part of a scandal, how simple it had seemed. She'd had no thought that Genevieve should do something so foolish as to sacrifice her happiness for Gillian. Now, she understood.

Because her nieces, they mattered. Their futures, they mattered.

In that, her father was not wrong in calling her out as selfish for failing to put them first.

A half-mad little giggle worked up her throat, the sound of it drowned out by the swell of the orchestra and the din of the jubilant crowd. One hated face stood out among the crowd, a flute of champagne dangling between his fingers that he waved about as he spoke with Gillian's father.

Hatred so sharp, so palpable coursed through her. For both of them. Accompanied by a deep hungering to cross over and scrape her nails over Lord Barber's reviled face, leaving behind a bloody trail.

Her mother gave her a sideways look. "You really should be more grateful," she said from the corner of her mouth. "He's willing to fix the mess you made."

"How *honorable* of him." Disdain pulled those words from her, though she could not sort out whether her mother spoke of her father or Lord Barber.

"Indeed it is," her mother said, either failing to hear or care about the sarcasm in Gillian's response. With that, the marchioness hurried over to join the circle of vile ladies she called friends. She stared on at the trio, and once more, she saw a glimpse of what her parents would have her future be. All for one mistake. All because of one night of recklessness that had cost her so very much.

Her gaze went back to Lord Barber alongside her father. And once more, she tasted a newly familiar rage.

That was their world, one in which an assaulter could live freely, unaffected by his crimes, while she was left picking up the pieces of her life. How everything would have been different had she heeded Honoria's urgings, had she not talked her friend into going. Had she not let herself be separated from her friend. Had she not drunk that champagne.

So many mistakes she'd made that day.

I should have never gone… I should have never gone…

The litany played out in her head, and she forced herself to look away from that hated face.

Her gaze landed on a tall figure descending Lord and Lady Grafton's marble staircase.

Her heart stopped.

Gillian blinked slowly several times.

Surely she was imagining him, because, really, he should be here now? Here, when he was so infrequently at the events hosted by Polite Society?

For one sliver of a moment, she let herself think that he was here because of her.

Only, this wasn't the first event he'd attended as she had.

Seven.

Seven other times, she'd seen him stalk in or through some lord's ballroom with long, purposeful strides, a notepad in hand as he met one person or another, and they hurried off for whatever business had brought him to the affair.

Of those seven events, zero was the number of times he'd come for Gillian. Or sought her out. Or even, for that matter, glanced her way.

She'd been, simply put, invisible to him. A friend forgotten.

Her toes curled sharply into the soles of her pinched satin slippers.

Despite all that, she'd still been pathetic enough to turn to him, because she'd not been able to bring herself to bother Genevieve because of mistakes Gillian had made. And she couldn't go to Honoria. Their friendship had not been the same since they'd parted after the masquerade.

Striding down the side of the ballroom, Colin scanned the room as he went.

Gillian noted an incongruity between Colin as he was now and as he'd been the previous seven events—he didn't have his notepad.

Then, from the opposite end of the dance floor and over the heads of waltzing partners, his gaze collided with hers.

And he stopped.

Over the years, Colin had seen Gillian Farendale in many ways. Clad in breeches she'd filched from one of her family's stable hands so that they could go fishing. Wearing a girlish frock muddied from her tumbling down the Cheshire hills.

Never had he seen her… like this.

Colin stood there. Riveted. Unable to move. Forgetting to breathe. Losing all words but one.

Magnificent.

She was gloriously gowned in a teal-green silk, the fabric shimmering in the heavy glow cast by the chandeliers overhead. The garment clung to her gracefully curved hips and accentuated the generous swell of her buttocks.

She was a siren of the sea, beckoning him.

And then, he reached her.

Gillian lifted a hand to her chest. "What—?"

"I came for you."

At that directness, her eyes widened a fraction, and her arm fell to her side. "For…?"

He held out his arm, and Gillian moved that still unblinking gaze from his elbow to his face and then back to his elbow.

He felt his neck flame hot as he waited, on display—

Her long, glove-encased fingers slid onto his sleeve, and some of the tension left him as he led her out onto the dance floor.

"You dance," she said as he settled his hand at her waist.

His fingers curled reflexively, lightly into that supple flesh. He made himself relax his grip, and as the orchestra began the set, he guided them through the movements.

"Surprised?" She had, of course, a right to that shock. As a bastard-born son—and worse at that, a bastard-born son who'd been rejected by his ducal father—there'd been no expectation that he should be possessed of those skills.

"Surprised I didn't know," she said softly, her steps as graceful as when she'd streak through the fields of dandelions to set the flowery weed dancing with that white snow. Her words yet again conjured shared memories of the only happy times he'd known as a boy… and now as a young man.

He lowered his head closer to hers, and under his touch, he felt her body tremble. Was it fear? Or something… more? Something in thinking it might be fear around him hit like a kick to the gut. Because of what they'd once had. Because of what someone else had wrought.

When he again spoke, he was careful to keep his lips from moving. "You left."

"I was going to have to leave either way," she said, her mouth also nearly motionless.

That skill, his and hers both, was the product of the effort they'd perfected to speak to each other across the village parish or on opposite ends of church pews.

They glided through the steps as he held her in a way he'd never thought to. And she, in his arms, felt right.

He stumbled.

Gillian clung to his arm, steadying herself.

"I never said I was a good dancer," he muttered, lying.

His mother, who'd dreamed of the day Ravenscourt would return for her, had practiced the waltz with Colin. Over and over.

"You're lying," Gillian said. "You are more skilled than any other man present."

He felt his cheeks warm.

Gillian waggled her eyebrows. "My goodness, Colin Lockhart, are you… blushing?"

"As I cannot see my cheeks, I could not otherwise say," he said flatly.

A laugh spilled from her lips, that joy-filled, unrestrained expression familiar and yet also different. As a woman grown, there were husky shades to that tone. And something shifted in his chest. "You are direct as ever, aren't you?"

"And you aren't."

Her smile slipped. "I told you I had to leave, and as such... I did." Just that. *I did.*

His gaze went across the ballroom to her father, that reviled figure who'd made Colin's nearly impossible life completely so. Heartless. Ruthless. Only, that gentleman wasn't the one who called his notice, but the younger, taller, more slender man alongside him.

In that instant, Colin came to two distinct realizations.

One, the man beside the marquess was none other than the one who'd dishonored Gillian. The one responsible for the desperation that had led her to seek out Colin.

And two, there was no way he was going to let her to that cad's machinations.

His mind balked and then raced.

"What is it?" Gillian asked.

Her question came from a distance, and he let it go ignored as his thoughts spun.

There were a thousand and one reasons not to consider the path his thoughts had wandered. His business was failing. He was to Birmingham. His responsibilities belonged to his sister and establishing a career that would see Colin fully independent. "I'll do it."

The place between her eyebrows puckered. "I don't...?" She gave her head a little shake.

"You said you are in need of a betrothed. I'll speak to your father tomorrow morn."

The music came to a stop, and as the couples drew to a halt around them and broke out into polite clapping, Colin bowed quickly and stepped around her. He quit the main hall and made his way down the empty corridor that led out to the main foyer.

The thin ivory runner in the hall only partially muted his footfalls.

He expected there should be a sense of panic as to what he'd agreed to. The decision to sign on as "pretend betrothed" to a lady of Polite Society was hardly logical and rational, everything he'd prided himself on being through the years.

But she was not just any lady of Polite Society. She was Gillian. And she was in need.

Gillian, who had been there for him, and—unlike Catriona, who had the protection of an army of brothers—she had no one. Other than the rake of a brother-in-law, she'd spoken—

A figure stepped into his path, and he brought his arm back reflexively. "Gillian," he exclaimed, swiftly lowering his arm. "What in hell? You don't just go about sneaking up on a man."

Gillian slid into his path. "That is it?"

It was his turn for puzzlement. "Is there something else you require?"

Her brows dipped.

Oh, he'd seen that menacing look before. A scowl worthy of terrifying the biggest, tallest bullies in Cheshire. Never before, however, had that menacing glint been turned Colin's way.

"My 'that is it,' Colin, referred to what you just said moments ago, not the favor I initially sought from you."

"Oh." He retreated a step.

Gillian followed.

"Furthermore"—she dropped her hands to her hips as she advanced—"you don't simply state that you're speaking to my father and then leave me in the middle of a dance floor... and then just leave altogether."

The back of his right knee caught the corner of a hall bench, halting his retreat. "Bad form?"

"The worst."

She stopped, so close that their toes kissed, her perfect satin slippers against his heavily scuffed black boots, which dwelled in the far recesses of his armoire, only to be pulled out and donned when he had a case.

Those two contrasting articles, pressed together as they were, once more illuminated the great station divide between them.

She'd always been beyond his reach. Then, as a friend. Now...

The thought ground to a screeching halt as he refused to let his mind finish a thought that was even more illogical than the decision to help her.

Gillian moved her gaze searchingly over his face. Her eyes serious. Intent, when they'd once been teasing.

In the past, she would have peppered him with more words and questions and challenges. No more. Of its own volition, Colin's hand came up, and he dusted his knuckles in a quick caress along the curve of her right cheek. Like the softest silk of a cravat his mother had spent her hard-earned coin on for his eleventh birthday.

"You're quieter than you were," he murmured.

"I've grown up," she whispered, her breath slightly tremulous as her chest moved with quickened respirations.

"Yes." His throat worked. "Yes, you have." They both had. They had lives of their own to live and circles they moved within. And the truth remained that those spheres would never intersect. They couldn't. Not beyond what he'd already committed to, and not more than what she'd asked for. It took a physical effort to bring his arm back to his side, breaking that contact.

Did he imagine the spark of regret in her eyes? Or was it merely a flicker of the lit sconce beside them? "I appreciate your offer of assistance," she said. "However, I've rethought my request, and..."

He stared dumbly at her. "And?" he prodded when she didn't finish.

Her jaw tensed a fraction. "And I'm no longer certain of—" She pressed her lips together and glanced over her shoulder. "I should return."

She'd... changed her mind? Just like that? Which would also mean... what, in terms of the gentleman who'd robbed her of her virtue?

A primitive fury pumped through his veins.

She thought to just go back to the ballroom?

The hell she was.

He stepped into her path, this time the one to block her escape. Reaching beside them, he opened the door of the nearest room and waited for her to enter. Allowing her that decision.

She stared at it for a long while before wordlessly entering. Colin followed in after her and drew the panel shut.

Crossing his arms at his chest, he leaned against the door. "Well?"

"I don't know what to do, Colin," she said on a furious whisper. All the fight seemed to go out of her, and she slid into the folds of a needlepoint slipper chair. Her skirts settled around her in a soft rustle.

This was how he'd never seen the always smiling Gillian Farendale, even when she'd been taking on his bullies. Now, she was lost, troubled. Unsmiling.

Colin took up the spot closest to hers, perching on the edge of a painfully delicate settee. "You're not thinking of marrying him."

It wasn't a question. Because the Gillian he knew, the same woman who'd boldly come to him, who'd gone toe-to-toe with his clerk, wouldn't entertain the possibility of tying herself to some cad.

"I wasn't." Gillian stared down at her interlocked gloves.

I wasn't. Not *I'm not.*

She twisted those digits together, eyeing them like they contained the truth about human life.

He covered them with a hand. Even through the soft leather, there came a rush of heat, the kind that sizzled and crackled on the cusp of a lightning strike.

At last, she looked up. "I have nieces," she said. Her gaze fell to the floor. "And it would be the height of unfairness for them to pay for my mistakes and sins."

Colin stilled. "That is what you believe?" She still insisted that she was responsible for what happened to her.

The graceful column of her throat glided up and down in an uneven rhythm. "It is what I *know*. It was my fault. I went to the masquerade. *I* drank that glass of champagne." So much regret and sorrow burned from her gaze, it hit him like a fist to the chest.

He brought their joined hands close to the place his heart was breaking. "You were deceived by a blackguard. He *is* in the wrong, Gillian. He robbed you of choice and he is the only one to blame. You have done nothing wrong." Colin gave her hands a light squeeze. "Nothing."

A tear slipped down her cheek.

Colin caught that lone drop on its winding trail. She squeezed her eyes briefly shut. "My father reminded me of my niece—"

"Your father can go to hell," he said bluntly, and a smile formed on her lips... before fading.

"But he's not wrong. Reputations, they matter for women. And if I place my own happiness and future first, then what of them? They're the ladies with a rake for a father—"

He dragged the settee closer so that their legs brushed. "That's not *your* crime."

"—and an aunt who was famously ruined at a wicked affair."

"That is not a crime," he clipped out, once more, willing her to see that. "*You*? You did nothing. The fiend responsible for violating your trust is the one to blame." He scraped a hand through his hair. How could he make her see that?

There was such a softening in her eyes. "The world won't see it that way, Colin. In their eyes, I went, and I sipped from that champagne, and therefore, the fault lies with me."

Yes, that was the way of Society. Possessed of so many different standards for the elite nobles, for everyone born outside those illustrious ranks, for the ladies among them.

"You *never* cared about what the world says, Gillian." It was why she'd been his only friend. When everyone else had looked upon him with disdain and scorn, she'd called them out for that cruelty and injustice.

"No, but I didn't have nieces to put first then."

"Would you want them to marry some cad?"

"They're babes, Colin."

"They won't always be," he reminded. "In eighteen or so years, they'll be any other lady moving amongst Polite Society. Would you have either of them marry some heartless cad to sacrifice another loved one?"

She frowned. "It's not the same thing." She made to stand, but he caught her hand. Giving it a light squeeze, he implored her to remain.

"Is it, Gillian?" He held her gaze. "*Is it?*"

What she contemplated, it was a decision that was irreversible, short of her or the gentleman's death. The decision would also spare Colin from fulfilling the request she'd put to him so that he might refocus all his attentions on his work. And yet, since she'd entered his life again, he'd not thought much about his assignments. Or Birmingham. Or business.

Instead, while thinking of her making this decision, he felt something wind through him, sharp and insidious, cloying, something that felt remarkably like jealousy. At the idea of her married to another man, a growl climbed his throat. And to the fiend who'd violated her.

He proved less heartless than he'd believed himself to be, for he could not just walk out of here this night, knowing she was even considering making that choice.

"Do you truly believe you don't deserve to have the ultimate decision as to your future?" he asked quietly. "Do you think your happiness somehow matters less than that of your nieces or anyone else?"

CHAPTER 11

WHEN SHE'D BEEN A GIRL of twelve, and she'd gone to visit Colin Lockhart's cottage, only to find it empty but for the meager furnishings his family had had there, she'd gone searching.

She'd asked questions of the parish vicar, who'd been smitten with Colin's mum.

She'd asked the closest neighbors they'd had.

She'd even inquired with the meanest, ugliest bully who'd brutalized him, and for it, Gillian, over the years.

To no avail.

It was as though he'd simply vanished.

She'd eventually quit looking, but she'd never stopped wondering. Or thinking of him.

And then, one day by chance, she'd read his name in the far back pages of a paper, the great constable Colin Lockhart. From that moment on, she'd followed his exploits. Every single one of them.

She'd learned of his reputation for being ruthless and single-minded in solving his cases. She'd heard tales of how feared he was by all who crossed paths with him.

Do you think your happiness somehow matters less than that of your nieces or anyone else?

The immediate answer had been: yes.

Yes, in fact, she'd thought her happiness mattered not at all because she'd blamed herself for what had happened that night.

If she'd not gone to the masquerade.
If she'd not been led off by Lord Barber.
If she'd not drank from that champagne.
So many 'ifs'… and they'd all consumed her.
She'd believed herself at fault… until this night.

Until Colin had helped her see that Lord Barber was the one to blame.

Colin, who could have simply accepted that she'd marry Lord Barber so that he could be done with her, and had instead, debated her; insisting that she deserved more. Nay, showing her that she deserved more of life.

And every last part of her heart was forever lost to Colin Lockhart.

But then, she'd always loved Colin. First as a friend and then as a girl whom he'd still not seen before him—not in a romantic way, that was.

I'm not to blame.

"You're not the hardened soul you'd have the world believe, Colin Lockhart," she murmured, palming his chiseled cheek.

Under her gloved palm, his flesh stood out a crimson red.

"And you're blushing," she whispered.

"Men don't blush."

She scoffed. "Of course they do. That's nonsense." She allowed herself one more light caress. "And it doesn't make you weak." It made him wonderful. Human and real.

His eyes glinted, dark flecks that sent her belly fluttering.

And then his gaze slid past her, beyond her shoulder.

She knew the precise moment he withdrew from her. He closed his eyes.

Gillian went cold, and her gut clenched. "Why won't you look at me?" she asked quietly.

He opened his eyes, and she drew in a shaky breath at the depth of emotion burning from those emerald depths. "Because I don't trust myself around you in this moment," he said sharply. "Because I want to kiss you, Gillian." The slight nob of his Adam's apple worked. "And because of that, I'm not different from—"

Leaning over, she kissed him, ending the remainder of whatever falsities he'd spill.

He stiffened, but that tensing lasted a half beat of her heart before he kissed her back.

There was a tenderness to the glide of his lips over hers, again and again, that grew in intensity, and she met his mouth. Returned that kiss.

She didn't even know if she'd ever been kissed. She had no memories of what Lord Barber had done. But this, having control of this moment and sharing Colin's embrace, carried a heady sense of power, one she'd been without. And she burned from the inside.

Not breaking their embrace, Gillian came to her feet and moved to the vee between his legs, and with her standing over him, Colin angled his head back, searching for more of her.

With a whispery sigh, she sank into him, curling her fingers into the smooth fabric of his wool tailcoat. And it was just so very right that she was doing this was this man, her childhood best friend. Her confidant.

Colin cupped her nape and angled her head, better availing himself to her mouth.

Her entire body quivered; heat sparked through her. The air all around them sizzled as every sense, every sensation heightened, leaving Gillian dizzy.

Moaning, she parted her lips, and Colin touched his tongue to hers, a bold brand that he lashed, gently at first and then with an increasing ferocity. There was a primitiveness to each glide of their tongues as they tangled together. He tasted of cinnamon and apples, an unexpectedly desirous melding.

She'd thought never to know this or feel passion. These past weeks, she'd known and felt nothing but shame.

And mayhap she should in this instant, too.

She, however, intended to allow herself only the splendor of this moment.

His hands came up and settled on her waist before he continued with that glorious slide of his hands over her, those fingers long and callused, and yet his touch so very gentle. He moved them along her arms with an infinite tenderness.

Gillian curled her fingers into the dark strands at his nape and brought herself closer to him, deepening their kiss. He groaned into her mouth, the reverberations thrumming within, and she laughed breathlessly, that sound swallowed by his mouth.

Their breath came in like spurts, with no clear delineation between them.

Her legs drained of energy, and she collapsed onto his lap.

All the while she slid her tongue against his, an ache settled between her legs. A hungering so painful that she lifted her hips reflexively in a bid to alleviate the sensation, somewhere between bliss and agony. A need… for more.

This was what she'd wondered about. Nay, what she'd wanted to know. The heady taste of passion, and she wanted it now, here, in Colin's arms. Because of his touch.

He drew his mouth from hers, and she bit her lower lip to keep from crying out at the loss, but his lips merely moved their search lower, along the curve of her jaw, down to her neck, lower still, to the dip in her bodice, that place where her heart throbbed.

And he stopped.

She sat there, panting, staring down at his bent head.

Don't stop.

Why had he stopped?

"Forgive me," he said, the somberness of his tones composed and steady and wholly at odds with her own thoughts, hazy and dizzy from desire.

She climbed from his lap and stood over him. "I don't *want* your apologies, C-Colin." Her voice faintly trembled. "I… wanted to kiss you."

Gillian braced for the rush of shame to come, like that that had followed the other wicked decisions she'd made before this. Only, it never came. Not from kissing Colin. There couldn't ever be regret in that. That had been her choice. Her decision. He'd made her see that.

Color climbed his cheeks, giving him an endearingly boyish look. He came to his feet. "Yes, well, per my reason for being here…"

Her. He'd come for her. Not business. Not a case. Her. And her heart swelled over for it.

"What would you do, Gillian?"

What would she do?

Gillian wandered away several steps, giving him her back.

Yet again, he put the decision with her. He believed her worthy and deserving of a choice her parents and most of Society would rob her of. One she'd very nearly let herself be robbed of. And very possibly would have had he not had her consider her future and what she would say to her nieces one day about their own decisions.

She faced him. "I would gratefully accept your offer of assistance."

Clearing his throat, he shifted them to a safer topic—the planning and timing of their partnership. "I've work in Birmingham."

She went absolutely still. Of everything he might have said next, that had certainly not been it. "You're… leaving. For Birmingham?"

He glanced about. "Tomorrow. Following my visit with the marquess." He tugged his gloves from his pocket and beat them together distractedly. Following her focus on that movement, Colin stopped and pulled the fine leather articles on. "The timing lends itself to our arrangement. My partner… and I," he made himself say, "are considering a move there. When it is time to sever our connection, it will be simple enough for you to balk at moving from London. We'll part ways, and then it is done."

It was… that simple. She'd have the benefit of a pretend betrothal with a betrothed who was not there. There needn't be frequent public displays of they two together. There needn't be events they had to attend in each other's company. Or interactions of… any kind.

It was, for what they intended, the perfect plan.

So why, despite the gift he'd offered, did she have this overwhelming urge to cry?

Because of the permanent move he spoke of. Because of the thought of Colin leaving when she'd only just found him.

"Does that work?" he asked when she still said nothing.

She started. "It does. Of course." It was, simply put, splendid. But she lied. It was… everything awful. "Thank you," she made herself tack on. "I should return to the ballroom."

"Yes."

She lingered for a moment and then started for the door. Gillian spun back. "Why did you change your mind?"

He answered with a question of his own. "Does it matter?"

Gillian considered that for a moment. "Yes. I think it does." She blushed. "Which I know is ungrateful, because I should be just appreciative of the fact that you have offered to provide assistance."

"Because you were my friend," he said quietly, moving closer to her once more.

"Were," she echoed, hugging her arms to her middle.

"Are," he murmured. "You *are* my friend."

Her heart thumped hard in her chest.

"I'll come by tomorrow morn."

Sweeping back over to him, Gillian went up on tiptoe and placed her lips against his cheek. "Thank you."

As she took her leave, she felt his eyes on her, following her movement, until she'd gone.

CHAPTER 12

THE DAY COLIN AND HIS family had been tossed out of their family cottage, the marquess hadn't seen to that task.

Given his birthright, Colin never would have merited any visit from the marquess.

Marquesses didn't pay visits to people like Colin.

No, when they had complaints or issues to address, they sent their servants.

In Colin's case, and as a result, in his family's case, it had been the man of affairs who'd arrived at his cottage. That exchange, between the gentleman servant and Colin's mother, had lasted no longer than eight, nearly nine minutes.

From that, they'd had until the next mail coach to get themselves out of Cheshire, with a threat of retribution if they were ever to return.

And mayhap, if Colin were being truthful with himself, at least in some small part, the decision to help Gillian was in some part because of the satisfaction it would bring Colin in helping her thwart that monster's wishes. The marquess found pleasure in controlling lives… and ruining them. He'd done it to Colin and his mother and sister. And now the heartless lord intended to do the same to his daughter.

But it wasn't all about revenge, or glee in denying Ellsworth the match he wanted for Gillian.

Which was why it was the ultimate irony that Colin now found himself being shown through the halls of that same distinguished nobleman's fancy Mayfair household.

Or mayhap it was, really, a triumph. This time, the marquess would have to deal directly with him. Now, there was no being sent away. Or there wouldn't be. Ellsworth had already attempted to do so, but Colin had made it clear to the butler that he had no intention of being turned away.

They reached the marquess's office. "Mr. Lockhart," the butler murmured and then backed from the room.

Seated behind his desk, his head bent over a book and a monocle to his eye, the older lord gave no outward reaction to Colin's arrival. "Shut the door behind you," he said to the head servant.

Lord Ellsworth didn't bother to pick his head up from his work or issue an invitation forward.

The marquess could still threaten him for his dealings with Gillian. But alas, Colin wasn't the same helpless boy he'd been. And furthermore, his business was already failing.

Birmingham...

It was just one more reminder that Birmingham made sense. He took a seat.

"You're the one, then," Ellsworth drawled in slightly nasally, flawlessly clipped tones.

He kept his expression cool. "My lord?" he said, refusing to give anything more.

"My fool of a daughter spoke of a... betrothed. And"—he peered down the length of a bulbous nose at Colin—"I take it that's you."

"I am," he said coolly.

Lord Ellsworth grunted. "My daughter is fanciful. Foolish. Rash. It is why she found herself in the position she did. You're aware of what transpired?" he asked, so conversationally that it took a moment for Colin to register exactly what Gillian's father had said. "He bedded her."

Colin's hands curled sharply around the gleaming mahogany arms of the chair, his nails leaving indentations that would forever mark this moment. "I don't care about that," he said when he trusted himself to speak.

Ellsworth snorted. "No one could believe that." Climbing to his feet, the marquess crossed to his sideboard and poured himself a glass of sherry. "Come now," he said, inserting a peculiar crystal stick, he proceeded to stir his drink. "What man would want to take the sullied goods sampled by another? Hmm?"

That tiny crystal stick knocked against the sides of the glass, an irritating *clink-clink-clink*. The marquess's actions, that grating sound, bespoke the man's indifference to Colin's presence. To the request he'd put to the hard-hearted lord. To Gillian.

This time when his hands curled reflexively, he forced them to relax. Drawing on the years of restraint he'd honed, he sat there, waiting. Refusing to reveal any of the volatile emotions that coursed through his veins.

The marquess tapped his glass several more times with the stick before removing it from his narrow-rimmed glass and returning it to the tray.

Sherry in hand, Gillian's father returned.

"I want to marry her," Colin said quietly when the other man took his seat.

Lord Ellsworth didn't miss a beat. "That's neither here nor there. A deal was worked out with Lord Barber."

Lord Barber.

His muscles tensed.

At last, the bastard had an identity.

Colin filed that information away. He'd deal with him.

Later.

"That may be," Colin said in even tones while the marquess sipped at his sherry. "However, it is not what Gillian wants."

The marquess's eyebrows snapped together, as over the top of his drink, he intently scrutinized him. "And… who *are* you that you'd refer to my daughter by her given name, Mr. Lockhart?"

It was then that it hit Colin. Why, the marquess had no idea who Colin was. His name, his identity, meant nothing to the all-powerful marquess. For all intents and purposes, Colin was a stranger to him. That realization should have set off rage. Ellsworth had destroyed the lives of his family, sent them away, and didn't have a recollection as to who he was. And yet, seated in the grand offices of the all-powerful marquess, Colin was capable of rage for just one person... for what her own father had done to her.

"I am her friend," he said when he trusted himself to speak.

He waited...for some indication that the other man might remember Colin and Colin's friendship with Gillian.

Lord Ellsworth snorted. "Men and women aren't friends, and"—as his glass dangled in his right hand, he flicked Colin's calling card at him with his left—"you? A mere 'mister' with no social standing would think to come here and expect that I'd gladly give my blessings for you over a viscount?"

"It is what Gillian wants."

Ellsworth chuckled. "Do you believe I care what she wants? This is a matter of what I want."

Colin froze.

This is a matter of what I want.

His detective's mind replayed the marquess' words from moments ago. *A deal was worked out with Lord Barber.*

Past tense, as in the exchange had already occurred.

But when? After the masquerade Gillian had attended... or before?

Colin stared intently at the man opposite him, watching him as he sipped at his spirits.

It was a sinister thought, lent credence by the experience Colin had in dealing with sinners... and in his knowledge of the extent of Lord Ellsworth's ruthlessness. A man who'd banish two children and their unwed mother to the unforgivable streets of East London was capable of anything.

"You coordinated it," he said quietly, calling the other man out.

The marquess looked at him over the rim of his glass. "These things are done all the time."

Rage. It clouded Colin's vision, briefly blinding him to the other man's visage before him.

"My last daughter proved recalcitrant in making the match I desired for her," Ellsworth went on, as if he'd not just casually stated that Gillian's ruin that night had been orchestrated. By her father. "It was a good match. An honorable one. She chose unwisely.

But"—Lord Ellsworth waved a hand about—"I didn't have high expectations either way where Genevieve was concerned. Just that she wed was enough."

And it spoke volumes for his disdain of that daughter that he'd freely share those details with Colin, a stranger to him.

"But my other daughter served a purpose."

There it was once again. Past tense, which revealed sinister plans the man had crafted for Gillian.

"What did you get out of it?" he asked, his voice a whisper coated with steel.

The marquess sputtered and thumped a fist on his desk. Colin's calling card jumped under the force of that strike. "How dare you? You come here and think to ask me all these questions? As it is, I granted you far more of an audience than you—"

Exploding from his seat, Colin lunged across the desk and dragged the other man over by his cravat, strangling him slightly. How was it possible this miserable, less-than-human monster before him had given life to one such as Gillian?

"What. Did. You. Get?" He bit out each syllable.

Ellsworth's eyes bulged, bleeding terror as he writhed and twisted.

Colin gave a tighter tug on that satin scrap.

"His votes before Parliament," the older man managed to croak, his voice garbled from fear and the hold Colin had upon him.

Colin's grip slackened. "You sold your daughter… for votes," he echoed dumbly.

Lord Ellsworth gave a shaky nod. "Important stuff that will preserve the East India trade."

The shameful company that, in spectacularly British fashion, had exploited an entire people for profit.

Color flooded the marquess' cheeks. "P-please," Ellsworth rasped when Colin held on to him still.

"That is what you traded your daughter's virtue for?" He'd allowed his daughter to be robbed of control of her body, all to manipulate her for his own ends. With a sound of disgust, he shoved the other man away, and the marquess collapsed into his seat, gasping for breath.

"I cannot renege now," Lord Ellsworth said in decidedly weaker tones as he rubbed at his throat. "She was too valuable."

Like a commodity. An item to be bartered, sold, and traded.

Fiery tendrils of rage wound through Colin's insides, and he took another step toward the marquess.

The marquess slunk farther into the folds of his chair, curled up like the coward he was.

He bent over the older man, relishing the way he whimpered and cowered. "My name is Colin Lockhart, and I was...and am, your daughter's friend. I am the friend you evicted from Cheshire."

Understanding sparked through the fear in the marquess's gaze. "You?"

He curled his lips in a cold sneer. "Me. And I am not a mere 'mister' with no social standing." Not any longer. "I have connections enough to ruin you, Ellsworth. Only...my connections? They are peers with power to rival yours, and my allies also include ruthless men who'd quite happily ruin a cur like you."

Before he did something, like kill the nobleman, Colin turned on his heel and stalked off.

All these years, Colin had hated his own father, believing there was no greater sin than ignoring the existence of a family he'd created outside of wedlock. He'd been so very wrong. Gillian's father... his response this day? This was far worse. Far more egregious. The height of evil.

And there was no way he was leaving her here.

But first, there was the matter of Lord Barber to see to...

CHAPTER 13

HER FATHER HAD REJECTED COLIN'S offer.

And that realization was a sign of how ignorant and foolish she'd been. Or rather, it was another mark of her naïveté that she'd believed her father would not fight her on that all-important decision. Since she'd made her come out, he'd been holding off for the best offer. He'd only ever seen her in a material light. Which match would be the most advantageous for him? For his prestige, his wealth. His power.

As such, she should have known he would have never accepted Colin's offer.

Thunder rumbled ominously outside as the steady patter of rain beat a staccato against Gillian's windowpane.

Lying in her bed, she stared up at the mural overhead, painted several years ago by her sister, who'd wanted to capture Gillian's favorite colors and place. Those shades of pale blues and pinks and soft white clouds conjured the country she'd so loved.

But there'd been something her sister had not included in the painting. Colin.

He had been the reason for Gillian's happiness there.

When she'd been a girl, her mother had lamented all of Gillian's many failings. All the while she'd committed herself to grooming Gillian for the future that awaited her—as the daughter who would make the ideal match for their family—there had been

Colin and the time together they'd had, exploring and playing games and imagining the futures they wanted for themselves… and each other…

Her gaze fixed on the ambiguous couple in the painting. A young lady in white skirts being pushed upon a swing. This painting, however, with the young man with that golden-haired lady, was different than the one in her hateful father's office. This one was joyous because of the couple there, together.

"You had better not marry Lord Thomas," Colin muttered, pushing the back of her seat and sending her soaring higher over the lake. *"He's insufferable."*

"He's nice enough." Gillian glanced back, sending the swing slightly askew as it rocked. *"Has he been mean to you?"* Because she'd knock him in the nose, she would.

"He's not going to appreciate you as you deserve, Gillian. Trust me."

Forcing her gaze away from that couple overhead, she looked out the darkened window. The rain came down harder, beating furiously against the window, like pellets striking the lead panes.

But then he'd gone, and life had sped along, bringing with it all the expectations that had inevitably been there waiting for her. A London Season. Suitors. Marriage. Or at least, continual talk of that wedded state. She'd no longer been able to escape it.

There'd been only duty and expectations in which her happiness had not been of any relevance to her parents.

Her lips twisted in a bitter smile.

Those same parents who'd sent away their eldest daughter, all because Genevieve's betrothal to a powerful duke had fallen apart. Through no fault of her own.

And mayhap Genevieve was the far better sister for having made the marriage of convenience, or so it had been at the time, with her husband, but Gillian… she didn't want to sacrifice herself. And she wasn't willing to.

In that moment of weakness with Colin, he had allowed her to see that her father was using Gillian's love for her family against her.

That was, mayhap, as much a gift as his willingness to play at betrothed to thwart her father's plans. Perhaps even bigger.

But he would leave on the morrow. And she'd never even had that last goodbye, though the way today had played out in her mind had included a meeting when he'd come to call.

The storm kicked up outside.

Plink-plink. Plink.

Another streak of lightning cut across the room, a bright flash of white that cast eerie shadows over her room. Shivering, Gillian drew her coverlet closer and stared at the rain coming down in slanted sheets, buffeting the window.

Plink-plink-plink-plink.

Something was striking the window.

Hail. Only, it wasn't. That sharp pinging…

She squinted.

Wait a moment…

Her gaze locked on the wide lead panes.

Those staccato pings weren't rain hitting the glass.

Shoving off her blankets, Gillian swung her legs over the edge of the bed. She hurried to gather her wrapper, and as she shrugged into the garment, she headed over to the windows.

Plink-plink-plink.

Rain hammered a more frenzied beat upon the glass.

Plink.

And there it was.

Gillian widened her eyes, and catching the window, she hefted it up.

Wind and rain pounded through the opening, slapping her face with the sting of water. Blinking back those drops, she leaned out.

Her heart forgot its job of beating.

Standing below, his black garments soaked, Colin cupped a hand over his eyes, shielding them from the rain.

"Colin," she said, his name lost to the forlorn howl of the wind.

He touched a finger to his lips and nudged his chin upward.

She shook her head.

"The…" he mouthed, but the remainder of what he said was impossible to make out.

Wiping the rain from her eyes, Gillian leaned farther out and peered at him.

All the while, the storm raged around them, and her plait whipped wildly about her.

"The win…" Lifting his arms, he made a gesture of shoving something up.

She puzzled her brow.

The window!

Pushing the window all the way up, she stared down at him.

And then horror hit her with the same force of the wind beating at her as he caught the metal bars along the side of the first-floor window.

He was going to scale it?

Her heart lurched as he hefted himself onto the first sill, and then with all the skill of a London pickpocket, he scaled the linear windows until he reached her sill.

Startled into movement, she backed away, allowing him to pull himself inside.

His feet hit the hardwood floor with a noisy thump. Every inch of his soaked frame, from his sopping black hair down to his black leather boots, dripped water, leaving a puddle about him. Then she registered… Colin was here… in her bedchambers. A very wet Colin, whose black garments clung to his frame, highlighting the contours of each muscle in his arms, the distinct bulges of his biceps, his triceps.

There was a masculine strength to his form that was absent from the dandified fops who didn't partake in physical activity and padded their garments to compensate for it.

Nor did shame come from her unwitting study of him. Any woman, of any station and any age, could only ever be held in silent awe of his beauty.

He doffed his cap. "I trust you have questions."

Yes, well, that would be the likely assumption about why she was standing there, gawking like a silent twit. Rushing into action, Gillian brought the window down. The rain continued to pelt the window.

"Wh-what are you doing?" she whispered furiously, scrubbing at her chilled arms. She didn't allow him a word edgewise. Gillian caught sight of his bruised and battered knuckles and gasped.

"You've hurt your hands."

"Not from climbing."

"Of course it is." Taking his cap from him, she caught his hands and raised them to study them. "I just s-saw you."

"I paid a visit to Lord Barber."

She stilled, her gaze locked on his injuries. "You..."

His jaw hardened. "He deserved what I dealt out."

The implication of that hit her.

He'd gone and beaten Lord Barber... for her.

Tears smarted. The only person who hated tears more than she was Colin. As such, she blinked those drops back.

He dusted his fingers along her jaw. "I don't believe he'll be deterred, Gillian. He is desperate for the funds he would receive through a match with you."

Colin was correct. And yet, she didn't give a jot in this moment about Lord Barber or his intentions. "I care far more about the fact that you are climbing buildings. You are going to get yourself killed, Colin."

He scoffed. "Of course not. I've scaled countless windows."

She eyed him quizzically. "As a detective?"

"As a street thief," he said flatly.

All the air went out of her, the sting of cold forgotten as she froze, absolutely numbed by his words. And she managed just one breathy syllable: "Oh."

Nay, that revelation highlighted the great gap between them. All those years they'd been parted, she'd not known where he'd gone or how he'd lived. And now she knew, and her heart splintered for it. "You became a street thief," she whispered, her voice shaking for reasons that had nothing to do with being soaked through.

He beat his cap against the side of his thigh. "An auspicious start for a detective indeed," he drawled.

But she was not fooled by that droll attempt at humor. His cheeks flushed. Not from the cold. No, she knew him. It was embarrassment. The honorable boy who'd lived in Cheshire would feel shame about that. Only desperation would have driven him to that point, and her heart broke all over again as she thought of what he'd endured.

Gillian drifted closer to him. "I know you. You would only have ever done what you did if you were required to. For your sister. For your mother."

A muscle rippled along the hard line of his jaw.

Of their own volition, her hands came up, and she dusted the remnants of the storm from him.

He didn't deny the truth of her supposition.

More questions about what he'd done in the years since their parting swirled. Her palm drifted up, cupping his sharp, chiseled cheek.

He trembled.

And she knew, with a woman's intuition, something else in that instant. That faint tremor had nothing to do with the cold and everything to do with her caress.

Drop your hand. Stop touching him.

Those directives born of common sense and propriety battered at her brain, but she was hopeless. She always had been where Colin Lockhart was concerned.

"I'm taking you with me."

She must have heard him wrong. "You're…"

That statement managed to knock her arm back to her side.

"And we leave now."

CHAPTER 14

ANY OTHER LADY WOULD HAVE wilted.

At finding him outside her window.

At his revelation that he'd been a common street thief.

At his announcement that he planned to take her.

And then, after wilting, any other lady would have raised the hue and cry for servants to see him tossed out.

But Gillian had never been like any other lady.

She'd not been like any person he'd known.

"I don't u-understand," she said slowly, rubbing her arms once more.

He needed to tell her. He needed to tell her the full extent of her father's betrayal, because she was deserving of all the truth. And then he needed to get her from this place.

He needed to get the both of them out.

"Colin?" Gillian's voice came hesitantly.

Moving past her, he started for the armoire, and pulling open the pretty painted ivory panels, he searched for linens. Row among row of gown after gown and dress after dress of all types and fabrics. And chemises, too. Delicate, lacy…

Bloody cad.

Muttering, he knelt and pulled out the drawers. "Where are your linens?" he asked as he rummaged.

"The linen closet."

Of course.

The linen closet.

Which was...

"In another hall," she murmured, her voice coming at his shoulder, indicating she'd moved nearer to him.

Yet again, of course.

Abandoning his spot at her armoire, he stalked over to her bed.

"Colin?" she asked quizzically as he yanked off her coverlet and pulled her sheets from the bed. "What are y-you—?" Her query ended as he whipped the sheet around her slender frame.

He proceeded to rub the moisture from her arms and back, patting her down. When his fingers reached the curve of her hip, sparks flared in the air between them. Crackling like the sturdy fire that blazed in the hearth across the room.

He made himself draw his hands back. "I'm taking you with me," he repeated.

She shook her head. "Where?"

"To Birmingham."

Silence met that pronouncement.

The fire hissed and popped in an offbeat tempo to the rain that pinged the window. "You... want me to go to Birmingham with you?" she asked tentatively.

"I..." He couldn't take her with him. Not truly. "I can take you along with me, until we figure out where it is safe for you."

As a detective, it was his duty to catch every detail. The way her white-knuckled grip clutched that togalike cloak wrapped about her.

"Oh."

The slight edge of hesitation in her tone gave him pause.

That was it: 'Oh'? For the first time since he'd left her father and resolved to take her from this place, he considered that she might not want to join him.

Not even a day ago, she had entertained marrying Lord Barber.

Now, he was asking her to risk her reputation... on him. Without even a fully crafted plan of what would happen next, he'd ask her to run off.

A bastard son of a caddish duke.

"Your father said no," he said, self-preservation requiring that he fill the void. "To my request. There cannot be a false betrothal."

But you can make it real...

His mind balked and jolted at the idea. Where in blazes had that even come from? He wasn't meant to be a husband. Because of who his father was. Because of the work he did. Before his courage deserted him, he made himself tell her all. "Your father was behind it, Gillian."

Confusion filled her features. "I don't...?" She shook her head.

His stomach muscles seized. How could he tell her this? How could he add more hurt to all she'd known? And yet, neither could he withhold that from her. "Your father coordinated with Lord Barber to see you... ruined in exchange for votes."

"Votes?" she whispered, her voice so very faint.

"Parliamentary votes," he added lamely.

Gillian went completely motionless and then her eyes, those windows into her soul, slid shut, but not before he'd witnessed the brief flash of agony within.

Colin would have crossed the room, and grabbed the poker from the hearth and plunged it through his chest if he thought he could spare her this or any pain.

Say something. Why wouldn't she say anything? She wouldn't even look at him. "I am so sorry," he said hoarsely. "I... debated whether or not to tell you, and decided you were deserving of the truth." What if that had been a mistake?

When she opened her eyes, all hint of sadness was gone.

"I always knew what he was," she said, with such matter-of-factness it proved more tragic than had there been sadness underlying that admission. "I knew he didn't value me or love me. As such, I am not shocked by that..." Her jaw tensed. "By his betrayal."

He touched a hand to her shoulder. "You deserved better." In a father. In the gentleman who would have wished to marry her.

"I did. And you deserved so much more in a father, too."

They both had.

How alike they'd been in that regard.

"As you predicted, Gillian, he's insistent that you wed Lord

Barber, and I'd sooner see the pair of them dead than—"

Gillian went up on tiptoes and kissed him.

It was a tender meeting of lips, so soft, so fleeting he might as well have imagined that butterfly caress.

When she sank back on her heels, she released the sheet, and it fell about them in a whispery heap. "Thank you." Racing over to the armoire, she made quick work of pulling out a valise tucked on the bottom shelf.

He stared on as she yanked out dress after dress and chemises and various other white undergarments. They all landed within that embroidered satchel.

She added a pair of boots and slippers and then headed for her vanity.

He strangled on his saliva when she drew out diamond-studded hair combs, a necklace, a bracelet, emerald earrings. Those pieces would have seen his family cared for, as well as his descendants, all while funding the establishment of his businesses. She stuffed those jewels into her bag with the same lack of care she had the articles of clothing, and then she popped up. "I'm ready."

He looked at her and struggled to swallow for altogether different reasons.

Her white nightshift was soaked through, and that cotton article clung to every curve of her, leaving nothing to the imagination, including the dark hue of her nipples, which pebbled beneath the fabric of the garment.

Colin abruptly turned and pressed a hand over his eyes. "No, you're not," he said. His voice emerged garbled to his own ears. "You cannot go out like that."

"Of course," she muttered, that matter-of-fact tone belonging to one wholly unaware of the effect she'd had on him. Or mayhap, it was one more sign of her trust in him.

His ears were attuned to everything, every subtle move of her body, as she strode back to the armoire. The wet fabric swishing noisily as she walked, the errant drip from her soaked plait as the excess water hit the floor.

Then came the slow rustle of fabric as she slid the garment from her frame, and the article landed on the floor with a shuddery whisper.

Behind his hands, he clenched his eyes closed even tighter.

This was… too much.

Colin swallowed hard and pressed his spare hand atop the other.

"It is redundant, you know," Gillian said, as casually as before.

He puzzled his brow.

"You've your back to me. You can't see anything."

But he heard. Oh, Lord, how he heard.

There came another soft rustle, and he concentrated on breathing before realizing she'd spoken to him, and even as she hadn't asked a question, he had to say… something.

In the end, he managed nothing more than three hoarse, incoherent words. "It is… just…"

"I've finished."

Thank—

"I just require some assistance with the buttons down the back."

And he was broken once more.

He'd buttoned her up countless times. And laced her. There'd been so many outings to explore Cheshire, when she'd had to change out of the trousers and shirts he'd lent her in place of the dresses she had to return home in.

That, however, had been different. So very different. Then, she'd been a girl, and he just a boy more concerned with whatever escapades they'd been up to.

"Colin?"

Giving his head a clearing shake, he forced his arms to his sides and made himself turn. Slowly.

She'd already presented him with her back. The pale blue fabric gaped slightly, revealing the delicate expanse of her back.

Colin directed his eyes to the mural above them and prayed.

For strength.

For a restoration of his honor.

For a clear head.

"Is everything all right?"

That hesitant question brought his attention whipping away from the pretty scene overhead and back to her.

Gillian cast a look over her shoulder, a question in her eyes.

"Fine," he lied. He cleared his throat. "Everything is fine." Nothing was.

But then, nothing had been fine since she'd come crashing back into his life. His work, which had served as the whole center of his universe, had become an afterthought. He'd been solely consumed by her. The thought of her. Her future. Her safety. Her happiness. And when he wasn't focused on any of that, he was lusting after her.

Gillian gave him another look.

Jolting back to the last request she'd made, he hurried over and drew the pale muslin dress closed. And as he set to work on the handful of pearl buttons, his gaze drifted to the slim expanse of olive-toned flesh revealed through the edges of her garment.

His hands shook, his fingers fumbling with the simplest task, one that he'd seen to countless times before.

His knuckles grazed over her back, smooth like satin but as hot as the fire that raged beside them.

His palms trembled all the more.

Colin directed his focus again to that painting, searching for a distraction.

"It would help if you were looking at them," she said gently, having no idea of the internal battle that raged within him. "The buttons."

He made himself look at the task before him, and his gaze locked with hers.

"It is just me, Colin," she said softly, simply.

Only, it had never been *just her*. She'd always been so much more... than everyone.

And mayhap her father had seen that, and perhaps that was why he'd banished Colin and his family.

She didn't say another word as he worked the buttons into their grommets, managing to get through the task by alternating his focus on her happy mural and the neat row of pearls.

"It is beautiful, though, isn't it?"

She was.

Burned, he released his hold on her.

He followed her eyes up toward the ceiling and the bucolic

scene that played out, a young lad pushing a girl in white skirts upon a wide wooden swing that drifted out beyond a crystalline blue lake.

"Cheshire." Only… He tipped his head farther back. Not just Cheshire. That faceless pair were very much like he and Gillian of long ago.

"Yes," she whispered, drifting closer, wafting her citrusy scent about him, a blend of oranges and lemons.

It took a moment to register that he'd spoken aloud.

"My sister painted it," she went on. "And… part of me has always thought she saw us in that pair, which she couldn't have. She didn't know the extent of our friendship, but whenever I look at it, I think of us."

I think of us.

He froze.

Us. That word linked them in ways that they never could have been… for too many reasons.

This was dangerous.

Her words had brought them closer to… things he'd no place thinking about.

"We should go," he said gruffly.

"Of course." Gillian hurried and fetched a wool cloak. The moment she'd clasped it, she reached for her valise.

Frowning, Colin took in her skirts and that bag she held.

She stared expectantly at him.

"I… ah…"

Her eyebrows came together in an endearing display of unease. "You've changed your mind."

"Of course not. It was my plan."

"Well, you can have second thoughts about taking me."

Colin stalked over to the window. "I'm not really stealing you, but rather, absconding *with* you." Or… that was the plan.

"Yes. Yes, that is true, but—"

He frowned and shot a look over his shoulder. "Can we fix on the semantics later, Gillian, and focus first on leaving?"

She immediately went silent. It was short-lived. "In fairness, *you* were the one to bring up semantics."

A laugh bubbled up in his chest, and he barely managed to suppress that expression of amusement. God, she'd always had that effect on him.

"You didn't think this part through, did you?" she predicted from behind him.

"What part?"

"How we are going to get out."

He felt himself coloring as he turned to her. "I thought of…"

Gillian folded her arms and gave him a look.

"I didn't think of the exit quite as much."

She patted his arm. "That wasn't so difficult, admitting you need help. It is really quite fine accepting help, Colin. That is why I came to you and you—"

"Gillian?" he said, impatient.

"Oh, yes. The escape." She lifted a finger. "We use… the door."

"The door," he said flatly.

She pointed, and he followed that long, perfectly manicured finger over to the white panel. "Several of them," she clarified. "That door, and then we'll avoid the servants' staircase and use the main halls and entry to the foyer."

"You're mad," he choked.

"The regular household servants are abed. My parents have also taken to their respective chambers. The second butler has relieved the first, and the second butler also has a taste for my father's sherry."

She… had thought it out. Better than he had.

Taking her by the hand, he scooped up her valise with his other hand.

And they left. Remarkably, using the very route she'd sketched out, past a drunkenly slumbering servant and right out the front door and into the rain… and at last, into his carriage.

"We did it." Her laughter came breathlessly, and there was triumph in her words and tone. That joy was infectious, and he found himself joining in.

He thumped the ceiling once, and the carriage lurched into motion, and they were rolling through the fashionable end of London toward the end inhabited by those outside the illustrious ranks of the nobility.

Their laughter faded into an awkward silence, broken only by the tempest buffeting rain against the carriage.

Gillian shivered, shifting several times on the bench.

Gathering up one of the carriage blankets, he swept it about her shoulders. He took the other and rested it on her lap.

She made a sound of protest and tried to remove the article. "You're soaking wet, too."

"I'm fine," he said. He'd endured far harsher circumstances. He'd never say as much, because he didn't speak about his past. Until tonight. Tonight, when he'd shared with her the measures he'd taken to feed his mother and sister, was the first time he'd freely offered any of that part of himself to anyone.

Gillian tried again to move the blanket.

"I said I'm fine," he said, resting a hand on hers.

She stopped. "Thank you, Colin," she said softly.

Unnerved by her thanks, he brought them back to where their focus needed to be.

"We need to find a place that is permanent for you to go."

Was a trick of the light responsible for the glimmer of sadness in her eyes? *You're seeing that which you want to see because you're falling under the same spell Gillian Farendale always had over you.* It was why he needed to be free of her as quickly as possible. "We've already said your sister is not an option, but you cannot stay with me, Gillian."

Even if I want you to. He froze. Where had that idea come from? He wanted to help her. He considered her a friend. It was only that. Nothing more. He coughed into his hand. "I've business in Birmingham, and even if I didn't…"

"I know," she said softly, fiddling with her damp skirts. "I… I do have options. I have friends. Other friends, that is." Other than him.

And yet, she'd come to him. She'd considered him as part of the same ranks as whomever those women were. Knowing that, knowing she'd still felt close enough to him to seek him out, left him discomfited.

"Who are your friends?" he asked. Oddly, the question came not from the need to pawn her off on others and relieve himself of the responsibility, but from curiosity about who she'd become.

"Well, there is Phoebe." A softness came across her features, a carefree, whimsical glimmer in her eyes as she spoke of people he didn't know, people who'd become part of her life after he'd departed from it. "She is married to the Marquess of Rutland."

His brows shot up.

"You've heard of him, I take it," she said with a smile in her voice.

"I have." All of Society, polite and otherwise, knew tales of his ruthlessness. Yes, Gillian was better off not going there.

"You misunderstand."

"I didn't say anything."

A wistful smile danced on her lips. "You didn't need to. I know how you think, Colin. You assume I didn't seek out Phoebe because of the man she's married to. But that isn't the reason. Lord Rutland is a changed man."

Colin snorted. "Men don't change. People don't change."

"You're wrong," she insisted, with her usual faith in people, when life proved people weren't deserving of that. "Either way. They travel often. They have several children, and yet, they take them with them everywhere."

There it was again, that wistful quality that he had heard and recognized. And her clear yearning unnerved him for altogether different reasons.

He cleared his throat. "Who are your other friends?"

"There is…" Her lashes swept low. "Honoria Fairfax."

That slight pause was palpable.

He searched his mind. The name meant nothing to him. "Is there something wrong that you did not seek her out? Instead of me?" As the words left him, he wanted to call them back because of what Gillian would assume he meant. When that couldn't be further from the truth.

She studied her joined palms for a moment. "Honoria is endlessly loyal. She would help me in any way that I require."

Colin waited for her to say more.

"And yet, you've decided not to go to her?" he gently prodded when she still said nothing.

Gillian steepled and unsteepled the tips of her fingers, forming little arches that she promptly flattened before constructing them once more with distracted movements. Suddenly, she stopped. "She was with me that night," she said, directing those flat words at her long digits. "She didn't wish to go. I convinced her. We became separated. She... was the one who found me and made sure I found my way home, but..."

Her features twisted in a paroxysm of pain that cut right through him like the shot he'd once taken to his shoulder.

Gillian shook her head. "She hasn't come around since, and I don't know if it's because she blames me for us being there, or for what happened to me that night, or—"

Colin settled a hand over her palm, and the panicky roll of her words ceased.

She drew in a deep breath.

"Who else?"

"There is..."

He stared at her when she didn't immediately finish that.

"Francesca."

Again, she'd spoken as though Colin should know.

And a lifetime ago, he would have, because they'd known everything about each other—their dreams and hopes and the sources of their regrets and resentments in life.

Gillian shivered, drawing the blankets closer about her. "She was first a friend of Genevieve's. She is utterly lovely. But Francesca's father recently passed, and on the way to a winter house party, she was stranded and came upon a gentleman, also alone... and..."

"They fell in love and are since married and living their best life together?"

Gillian frowned.

He snorted. "I'm right, then."

She kicked him across the carriage.

He grunted. "What was that for?"

"For being cynical. I'll have you know they are very much in love, and I... didn't wish to bother them. Francesca would wish for me to come, though. I know that now."

It was settled then.

"You'll go to Francesca's, then. To happily-ever-after-ville."

The matter was resolved. They had a plan that would free her of her father and him of responsibility… and should have left him with a sense of relief.

Something, anything, other than this peculiar void of emptiness.

They didn't speak the remainder of the way to his townhouse.

When they reached the front, he pushed the carriage door open and took her valise.

He stretched his other hand inside and helped her down. Together, they raced the remainder of the way up the seven steps, and he fumbled for the key in his pocket. The small piece of metal slipped from his fingers and hit the pavement.

Almost as one, Gillian and Colin fell to a knee and searched around the growing puddles for the item.

The rain hammered down in slanted rivulets, and as she searched her fingers about, he was briefly riveted by how the drops clung to her endless golden lashes and the water slicked her face. She was the same siren who'd enthralled him.

Her eyes lit as she fished the key up from the puddle. "I have it," she called loudly over the storm.

What in hell?

Jumping up, Colin reached for her hand, but Gillian was already on her feet and had the key inserted and the door open. She swept inside, as bold and sure as if she were herself the owner of this place. Colin followed close at her heels, and with the heel of his boot, he pushed the door shut.

Motioning for her to follow, he ushered her to his bedchambers.

She didn't hesitate as she stepped inside, the evidence of her faith and trust in him humbling. Shrugging out of her wet cloak, she was careful to rest it over the metal floor by the hearth, taking care not to mar his floor, a consideration he'd never known from anyone of her station. Yes, his brother had married a lady, but Colin's sister-in-law was a woman who'd also lived outside the peerage in the country.

Gillian had been born and bred to High Society and had only ever treated him as an equal.

She continued her turn about his room and then stopped beside the tub. "You had a bath prepared?" she said softly, skimming her fingers along the top of the water, sending a little ripple across the smooth surface.

His neck heated. "I had my brother see to it. I anticipated that you would require it," he finished lamely.

A little smile teased the corners of her lips as she rejoined him nearer the front of the room. "You anticipated all," she murmured.

"With the exception of our escape, yes," he said dryly.

She laughed, the throaty, husky, unapologetic laugh that gave way to the little snort that punctuated her mirth, and he stared on, transfixed once more.

Her merriment stopped. "What is it?"

"I forgot what it was to hear you laugh." Just as he'd forgotten what it was to feel that emotion himself and freely share it.

"You always teased me for my snorting."

"I was a fool," he said quietly. "It is splendid."

Before he knew what he was doing, he was reaching for her at the same moment she reached for him.

Her lips found his.

Gillian stretched her arms up, twining her hands about his neck, twisting them in his hair.

"I don't want to take advantage of you," he said between kisses, wrestling for restraint.

Gillian drew back a fraction, and his chest lurched at the loss of her.

She took his face between her hands. Desire... nay, something more, some emotion that scraped him raw inside, and reminded him what it was to feel. "You cannot take something that is freely given."

I am lost...

"And I am found," she whispered and kissed him once more.

Gillian nibbled at his lower lip, taking that flesh between her teeth and lightly nipping.

Groaning, he slid his tongue into the hot, moist cavern of her mouth, and their flesh danced in tandem.

She whimpered, and that heady sound of her desire sent little reverberations through his mouth.

Colin roved his hands along the curve of her waist and lower to the generous swell of her hips. It wasn't enough. His lips needed to know all of her.

They moved, him guiding her back until the mattress met her knees. Clinging to the front of his still-soaked shirt, she drew him closer, and he would have followed her into the flames of hell for a fiery waltz if she'd so beckoned.

Carefully bracing his elbows on either side of her, framing her between his arms, Colin trailed a path of kisses down the curve of her cheek.

She moaned, her fingers curling in his hair. "I-I trust I a-am as shameful as my mother a-accused, b-because I've never felt a-anything like this."

Colin paused, his breath ragged as he drew back enough to hold her gaze. "There is no shame in you taking passion where you would have it."

Her eyes softened, and then leaning up once more, she kissed him.

Desire coursed through him, a burning need that, with every stroke of her tongue against his, jolted to his belly. His shaft ached, throbbing against her soft belly, the fabric of their garments a barrier that added a level of eroticism to each slide of their bodies against each other.

"You are beautiful," he panted, trailing his lips along her neck.

She moaned, long and endless, fueling this hungering for her. "You were of the opinion that girls were gross."

"I was a boy and an utter fool." He lightly suckled her flesh, pulling a little sigh from her.

Claiming her mouth once more, he glided his hand up, finding and cupping her right breast in the palm of his hand.

He groaned.

He'd never felt like this…

Colin's heart beat hard against his chest, that sound filling his ears.

Thump-thump-thump.

No, that was not his heart.

He ripped his mouth from hers.

Knock-knock-knock.

There it was again, not the pounding of his heart, but a knocking at his door.

And just like that, the moment was shattered.

Gillian's breath came quickly, and desire lifted from her eyes to be replaced with horror.

Colin jumped up.

He'd expected the marquess would know that he was the one behind Gillian's flight, but he'd not expected that discovery would happen until the early-morn hour at worst, the early-afternoon hour at best.

She pressed trembling hands to her cheeks.

"Lock the door behind me," he said quietly, and he headed for that incessant thump.

Colin found his way to the door. Pausing a moment to school his features, he waited, and when there was a break in that knocking, he drew the panel open… and froze.

He stared dumbly at the figure standing there, his garments even more soaked than Colin's.

His brother Vail grinned wryly back. "Generally, given the nature of the weather," he shouted into the tempest, "this is where one's brother would allow the other entry."

Colin tripped over himself in his haste to let Vail in.

Vail, Baron of Basingstoke, a great war hero and businessman, had located Colin in his pickpocketing days and saved him from that path of criminality he'd been forced upon.

"I understand you made an unexpected appearance at a *ton* event," Vail said.

Colin tried to resist the urge to move under that probing gaze.

"Given the amount of time you've spent urging me to take part in societal events, I thought you should have approved," he said as he went to pour himself the now-cold mixture of tea and coffee Gavin had left for him.

All the while, he was aware of Vail's gaze following him. Nay, studying him.

Careful to keep his features even and reveal nothing, he poured two glasses and handed one over to Vail.

His brother took the cup and sipped, giving not so much as an outward grimace at the sharply bitter taste. "Gavin's work, I take it?"

He nodded.

"I've something similar. Coffee and brandy." Vail set the glass aside. "It's not the affair I take exception with, but your reason for being there."

It would never be so easy that they'd leave it at discussing their brother Gavin.

Colin tensed.

He'd come to guard his secrets and the story of his past from anyone. Vail, however, was the only one aware of the circumstances surrounding the eviction of Colin and his family from the marquess's estates.

Vail lifted an eyebrow. "You've nothing to say?"

"You're making assumptions not based on any reality."

His brother snorted. "An assumption is something accepted as true or as certain to happen, without proof, and I'd say, given your past with the marquess, there is fact to my supposition."

Colin couldn't resist a glance toward the door to his bedchamber, where Gillian remained. When he looked back, he found his brother's eyes narrowed upon him.

"Is there?"

"Revenge?" his brother asked bluntly.

He bristled. "Of course not." Was that the manner of person his brother took him for? Except... he'd already revealed too much. Colin immediately clamped his mouth shut.

It was too late. Vail leaned forward in his chair.

"Then what is it?"

"It is simply..." Only, there was nothing simple about it. Not where Gillian was concerned. Not where she'd ever been concerned. The world they'd been born to hadn't allowed anything simple between them. "I was attending a damned ball," he finally said. "Leave it alone."

"I'll not," Vail said quietly. His brother carefully removed his damp leather gloves and rested one atop the other. "I remember how I found you."

Unable to meet his brother's stare, or confront those memories, Colin forced his gaze to the top of Vail's head. *Let it go. Let it go.*

I'm hungry, Colin. I'm so, so hungry.

His sister's piteous voice of long ago played all over again inside his head.

And he wanted to clamp his hands over his ears to drown out... all of it.

His brother proved unrelenting. "I remember how you were struggling and what you were doing in order to survive, because of Ellsworth."

A muscle twitched aggravatingly at the corner of his eye.

"And I'll not let you involve yourself with his daughter. Not when it will only see you ruined."

That brought his attention snapping back. He glared at Vail. "I'm a grown man. You offered your help years ago. I took it. I asked you to help Catriona. But now..." Colin jammed the tip of a finger into the grooved surface of his table, accentuating his point as he spoke. "This time? I'm not asking for your help."

His brother's face contorted; a twisted expression of worry and grief. "Of course I would help you. Whatever support might come from my name, or my connections, are yours. But that doesn't mean he won't try to ruin you... and hurt you."

"He can't," Colin said coolly. "Not anymore."

Vail gave him a pitying look, one that Colin strained to meet. "You cannot possibly believe that," his brother said with the same gentleness he'd used when he'd cornered Colin down an alley and cajoled him to stop running so he could explain their connection. "He didn't want you dealing with his daughter when you were children. Do you think he's going to suddenly prove magnanimous towards any relationship between the two of you now that you're grown?"

No. But there was no relationship. Not one that existed beyond him helping her to get away from Lord Barber and London.

And then his work would be done.

And you'll never again see her. She'll be even more removed from you than the separation imposed twelve years earlier.

That realization slammed him square in the chest, robbing him of breath.

For somewhere along the way, this willingness to help Gillian had become about… more. Things that were dangerous. Feelings he had no place having. Not with his work. Not with her origins. Not with—

"Colin?"

His brother's voice startled him back to the moment.

"Hmm?"

"Your business is already suffering, Colin." Thunder rumbled in the distance, an ominous exclamation point to his brother's not untrue statement. "It's why you're considering relocating all your services to Birmingham. With his power and influence, Ellsworth will attempt to quash those opportunities. He won't succeed, but neither will it be… painless, whatever he attempts."

"I'll not change my mind," Colin said between tightly clenched teeth. "I intend to help her."

A flash of lightning lit up the kitchens, followed by another loud crack of thunder.

His brother glanced around the kitchen, and his gaze lingered for a moment beyond Colin's shoulder on the door to the bedchamber, and for one moment, Colin believed his brother knew. But then, with a sigh, Vail stood. "You won't do that which you need to do to help yourself."

Cut ties with Gillian. His brother didn't say it, but his meaning was clear.

"I know what I'm doing," Colin said, coming to his feet and following his brother to the entrance of his residence.

When they reached the front door, Vail jammed his wet hat atop his head. "I hope so, Colin. I very much hope so." His brother stole another look back, but his features were completely unrevealing as Colin opened the door, and Vail stepped outside.

He stared on for several moments as Vail bounded down the steps toward the waiting carriage.

Colin quickly closed and locked the door.

Since Vail had found him on the streets, his oldest "found brother" had set himself up as his protector. In fairness, he'd really set himself up as the protector of all the Ravenscourt bastards he'd found. Having cared for his sister and mother following their eviction, Colin understood and had always related to that devotion. It was a shared bond that he had with Vail. And yet, as grateful as he'd forever be for the fate Vail had saved his family from, there still came the sting of resentment at those warnings.

At being judged.

He would give *Colin* advice?

Vail, of all people, who'd given his heart to a housekeeper who'd been sent into his household to steal from him. Granted, the pair had since fallen hopelessly in love.

Or mayhap the advice he'd given came from the mistakes he'd made.

And what was more, mayhap his resentment came from the fact that, in a place not so very deep down, he knew his brother was right to warn him of the danger posed by any and all dealings with Gillian.

CHAPTER 15

SHE HAD NOT LOCKED THE door behind him.

After all, she'd never been one to hide. And certainly not one to do as she'd been instructed... by anyone. Quite the opposite.

Her lips formed a bitter smile. Ironically, that was why she found herself in a quagmire. Then... and now.

Facing the window, she stared through the slight gap in the curtains at the street below as Colin's brother boarded his carriage and left.

It hadn't been her place to listen.

But she knew the level of her father's ruthlessness and had gone to the door to be sure Colin was all right. She'd intended to retreat after recognizing the baron. But she hadn't.

And, after eavesdropping on the exchange between him and his brother, she was the one who was not all right.

And she'd never be all right again. Not after that revelation between the brothers in the kitchen.

Lightning slashed in a zigzagging bolt across the London sky.

The baron's words rumbled through her head, as loud and as real as the thunder that shook the foundation of the house now.

I remember how you were struggling and what you were doing in order to survive, because of Ellsworth.

He didn't want you dealing with his daughter when you were children. Do you think he's going to suddenly prove magnanimous towards any relationships between the two of you now that you're grown?

Gillian wrapped her arms around her middle.

Her father had ruined Colin.

He'd destroyed him, forced him from Cheshire, that place he'd so loved. And what was worse, he'd forced Colin into a life of thievery. Colin, who'd barely had anything in Cheshire and had still given portions of his own food to other hungry boys and girls in the village. And even when she'd snuck bread and cheese from the kitchens so he might eat that instead, he'd still taken the smallest piece and given the rest away. To his sister. To his mother.

Tears burned her eyes.

It was too much.

There could be no recovering from this, the pain of what had been done to him because of her.

And... their relationship. That could never recover either. He'd known that, too. That's why he'd disappeared and never sought her out, even when their paths could have and had all but collided at various *ton* events. She'd expected he'd mayhap forgotten her. Or that he was too consumed by the important work he did. All the while, she'd just been naïve, blind to the extent of her father's villainy and evil.

She heard his approach and tried to will him to keep walking past her door.

Because she was a coward. Because she wasn't ready to see him. Nor did she think she ever could, not with the past laid out as truth between them.

She didn't want to confront what her father had done to him and his family.

She didn't want to think about all the struggles he'd known... all because of her.

And she didn't want to think of the level of her selfishness in coming to him for help.

He knocked.

In a prolonged moment of cowardice, she wanted to ignore that request. Let him think she was bathing or sleeping.

But she couldn't. Because he deserved her apology and her ownership of what had been done to him.

"You may enter," she called.

There came the faint squeak of rusted hinges as he let himself inside.

Still unable to look at him, she stared out the window at the place his brother had been just moments ago.

I'll not let you involve yourself with his daughter. Not when it will only see you ruined.

"You haven't bathed," he murmured.

She gave her head a slight shake.

The wide planked floorboards ceased groaning, along with the rustle of fabric, indicated he'd stopped. "You heard."

Gillian nodded.

"How much?" he asked quietly.

Misery formed a knot in her throat. "Enough." All of it. She'd heard… all of it.

There was a long pause. "I'm sorry you heard that."

Gillian's eyes slid shut. He would… apologize to her? Why must he be so very perfect in every way? She rested her forehead against the cool windowpane. "I'm sorry I didn't hear it sooner."

She felt him so close, and when she opened her eyes again, she found him just at her shoulder.

Nearly touching, but separated still.

Separated by so, so much.

"Why didn't you turn me away?" she whispered.

"You are my friend."

Just that. Spoken so simply and so instantly. *You are my friend.*

"Were." She repeated his earlier response to her, her voice catching. That past tense now made so much sense. Her father had killed their friendship. What she and Colin had shared died the day he'd been cast from his cottage and into the wilds of East London. Gillian's throat moved convulsively. And she'd so naïvely questioned why he could so easily dismiss those years they'd been friends. Again, Gillian hugged her arms around her middle.

"Don't do that," he said sharply.

She shook her head. "I don't…"

"Don't take on your father's sins as your own."

"But they *are* mine." Her voice came pleading to her own ears.

"He insisted I not see you and—"

"And you defied him."

Her throat closed up. "Precisely." She managed to squeeze that word out. "My selfishness—"

He took her gently by the shoulder and guided her around so she had no choice but to face him. "Look at me... please." That one word—*please*—was a request that empowered her. When the man who'd given her life had only ever ordered her about, and another man had robbed her of her virtue while she slept, Colin had only ever presented her with choices and decisions.

She lifted her gaze to his.

Emotion blazed from those irises that didn't know whether they wished to be an amber shade of brown, hazel, or soft green.

"Your friendship was the only spot of damned light that existed in my otherwise dark world, Gillian."

And she had confirmation of that which she'd only suspected before this moment. "That is why you did it," she whispered as his abrupt about-face finally made sense. "You were... repaying me."

"Yes." He winced. "No. Damn it..." He dragged a hand through his tousled locks, tossing free errant drops of rain that still clung to those strands.

He might forgive her. Because that was the manner of man he was. He was too honorable, too good to ever hold her at fault... which he should. Which anyone else would have.

And now, his business was in peril, and her father could, and would, just ruin him if he suspected she was here. Her breath came quickly. She had to go.

She took a step around him.

Colin matched her movement.

She made to go the opposite direction.

"Shall I take you to Francesca's tonight? Right now?"

"I don't know."

She no longer knew the right course or where to go. She'd sought to avoid being a burden to her sister and brother-in-law. She'd not been able to turn to Honoria. In every way, she'd been a burden, and she'd only just put that burden on another, on Colin.

She'd never wanted to be a chore to him, and yet, that was what she'd made herself.

"Initially, I did," he said. "Initially, I felt a sense of obligation to understand what danger you faced." He guided her chin up, his knuckles an unintended caress upon her skin. "But then I remembered."

Her heart caught at the emotion reflected in his eyes. "Remembered what?"

"Us," he said, not missing a beat. But that organ in her chest did. "I remembered what we'd shared and how it felt to be with you and to be close… with someone. You were right." His voice hoarsened. "I have been singularly focused on my work."

She'd not allow him to take on guilt. She'd been wrong. So very wrong. Only, she'd not known what had driven him… until now. "It was wrong of me to pass judgment upon you without understanding your circumstances." She blanched, recalling all over again that those sacrifices he'd made had all been a product of her father.

He flicked her arm. Just like he'd done when they were children and she'd been woolgathering instead of attending him.

"Ouch." More shocked than hurt by the gentle tap, she rubbed at the offended spot. "What was that—?"

"You're doing it again. Blaming yourself."

The last thread she had on her control snapped. "Well, you *should*. I passed judgment upon you, when all along everything you'd done was to care for those you love." The mother whom he'd adored. The sister he still looked after. "He threw you out. Drove you away because of me," she cried. All the energy went out of her, and she sank onto the edge of his bed.

The mattress dipped as he claimed the place beside her. "When I was ten, do you remember what I said to you?"

He'd said so much to her. They'd shared so many stories and dreams and laughter and wonderings.

"One of the first things," he clarified.

"After you told me to go away?" she mused aloud. Her wistful smile fell. "You told me no good could come from a marquess's daughter keeping company with a bastard-born son."

"And do you remember what you said?"

I don't care who your father is. I saw you defending Bertie Stent, and I would prefer to have a friend like you.

But even then, she'd missed the point. Her gaze caught and held on her damp skirts, the fabric marred with what looked like misshapen teardrops. What he'd said hadn't been about what she'd wanted in terms of a friendship. It had been about what peril he faced in having a connection with her.

Colin edged closer. "You don't understand what I'm saying," he said quietly. "You are misinterpreting, once more, because of misplaced guilt." He slid his hand over hers. "If you hadn't persisted, if you'd gone off that day because you were a marquess's daughter who believed I was right and that the children of the peerage had no place mingling with people outside your ranks, I would have never had a friend. I would have never had a reason to smile, and I wouldn't have known a bit of the joy I did during the time I was in Cheshire."

Gillian caught the flesh of her cheek between her teeth.

Colin stood, and she came to her feet beside him.

"We'll leave tonight… if that is what you wish."

Once again, he put her future in her hands. He'd aid her with whatever course she settled on. She warred with herself, with the risks that came with him helping her. To his business. To his reputation. "I promise I'll repay you."

His expression darkened. "I'm not seeking repayment," he said coolly.

"Of course. That isn't… I… I'm sorry."

He paused. "Should I… help you?"

She stared quizzically at him.

He blushed.

He, Colin Lockhart, great detective, formidable investigator, blushed, and it was endearing and boyish, and her heart moved in her chest.

She turned, giving him her back.

Colin immediately looked skyward and reached for her buttons at the same time.

Gillian angled herself so that she faced him, covering his hand with her own.

"I trust you, Colin," she said softly. And she did. She trusted him implicitly. Even as she knew the ugliness some men were capable of, she knew this man more.

She gave him her back once more.

His hands shook slightly as he worked her buttons free, and she felt that slight tremble against her back.

Her dress sagged, and she immediately caught it to her chest, holding the garment close.

"There," he murmured, and he took several quick steps away. "I'll leave you to your…" His gaze slipped over to the bathtub. He blushed again. "Yes, well…" he croaked, and spinning around, he left.

Gillian stood there, faltering. Warring between that which she wanted and that which was in Colin's best interest.

She closed her eyes. Why must he do this? Why must he make her fall in love with him all over again?

Her chest hitched as the earth seemed to sway.

Gillian's fingers came up, and she found one of the grooved mahogany posters of his bed to keep herself standing.

She loved him.

Mayhap that was why, all along, that she'd gone to him. Because in light of that great horror that had been visited upon her, the darkness of that moment, she'd needed him.

Because she'd known he'd not judge her. And she'd known he would support her unconditionally. And simply, she'd missed him. She'd missed him so much.

Just as she knew that the minute he took her to Francesca's and went on his way for Birmingham, she would miss him forever, and this time her heart would never recover from the loss of him.

CHAPTER 16

They left for Francesca's the following morn.

With the storm still raging, Colin joined Gillian in the carriage that he would then take onward to Birmingham.

Seated with his work spread out on the bench beside him and his notebook on his lap, he considered the paperwork his partner had assembled for Colin's upcoming meeting.

Or he tried to consider his work.

Since he'd boarded the carriage behind Gillian an hour and fifteen minutes earlier, he'd been impossibly distracted.

Of course, that was always the effect she had upon him.

First, as a boy seeing to tasks in the stables and gardens of his family's cottage, unable to focus on that work when she'd dangled the possibility of going off to explore with her. He'd accepted the help she'd offered, even as she'd been a marquess's daughter, all so he could finish his work sooner and follow her on whatever escapade she'd planned.

And now... as a man.

Only, this time, she didn't cajole.

He stole a glance over at her.

A book rested open but facedown, forgotten, on her lap as she stared with bald interest at the papers on Colin's lap.

Frowning, he drew those articles protectively closer, that reaction a product of years of carefully guarding his work and less a response to who she was.

Undeterred, she edged closer. Making no effort to conceal her intentions, she craned her neck, arching that long, graceful column to better avail herself of his pages. She boldly read his work, giving no indication that she was even aware of the fact that he watched her as she did.

Colin snapped his book closed and cleared his throat.

Reaching beside her, Gillian gathered her reticule and fished around. She withdrew a tin and removed—

"What is this?" He looked from her outstretched palm to her face.

"A comfit." She waggled her fingers, urging him to take one. That little motion sent the items within the tin clattering against the sides.

"A comfit?" he repeated dumbly.

"They're mints."

"I know what they are," he said slowly. "Why are you offering me one?"

"Something was in your throat."

"No, there wasn't. I was making a point that you were reading my work."

"I know," she whispered, a glimmer in her eyes. She waggled her offering once more, and this time he took a comfit. "From what I saw, it isn't a case. More's the pity." She muttered that last part under her breath. "Is it truly so secretive?"

"Yes. No. Yes."

She cocked her head. "Which is it?"

"It's... private," he said, reorganizing the materials on his lap.

"Do you fear I'm going to share your work with others or steal it for myself?"

Of course not. That was the immediate answer. But... sharing *anything* went against everything he was. "My work has required that I maintain a level of privacy."

"You don't discuss any of your work with Catriona or any of your other siblings?"

"No," he answered.

Gillian rested her chin on her hand. "It sounds as though your life has been very lonely, Colin," she said softly.

It had been.

That silent confirmation slipped around in his head, unsettling him. He wasn't lonely. Why... why... "I have a partner." He dealt daily with Roarke and discussed any number of things with him. Granted, matters surrounding his cases, but nonetheless, they *spoke*.

"I trust the two of you primarily speak on affairs related to your work," she rightly predicted. "Do you discuss regrets when cases are not solved as you wish or thoughts about the men and women whom you are helping?"

He glanced briefly out the window, where the rain continued to fall. "I don't really think of my clients... in that way."

"In what way?" she asked gently. "As human beings?"

"Exactly," he said, bringing his gaze back to hers. "The moment my relationship with a client becomes personal, that's the moment I'm unable to separate emotions from doing what I have to do to solve their case."

There was a prolonged silence, a wholly unfamiliar situation with Gillian Farendale.

"I assure you, my life is quite full," Colin said when she still didn't speak. "My days and nights are—"

"Full?" she supplied for him. Gillian lifted a perfectly arched, whitish-blonde eyebrow.

His neck grew hot. She'd make it out as though his life wasn't complete. And it was. He had everything he wished for. And needed. Granted, his business wasn't thriving, but he'd deliberately sought to build a life where...

Where you couldn't be hurt again?

Where you didn't suffer the loss of friends, as you did with Gillian?

Where you saw your sibling as an obligation to be cared for, because that made it easier than thinking about the ways you did and might fail her again?

Unnerved by those realizations buffeting at his mind, he looked down.

"Your days are filled with your plans for moving to Birmingham?" Gillian asked.

He nodded. This was safer. Details about his business didn't have anything to do with his personal connections... or lack thereof. "They're not my plans. The move is merely what my partner is suggesting that I consider because—"

He'd been wrong moments ago. This wasn't easier. For, try as he might, Colin couldn't bring himself to finish the remainder of that. He couldn't acknowledge that, for as successful as he'd been as a Bow Street runner, he'd proven disappointing as proprietor of his own business.

"Because?" she prodded.

"My business has not proven..." He grimaced, struggling to get out the whole truth. But mayhap it was because this was Gillian, with whom he'd once upon a lifetime ago shared his hopes and regrets and disappointments, that he found himself finally able to share. "My business has not proven as successful as I had hoped."

"It is a new venture, Colin." She laid a hand over his, her touch soft, gentle... calming. "That you have had the clients you've had with the competition you do is a triumph that you should celebrate."

Her words went against everything he'd viewed in terms of life. He'd not looked at his work in those terms she suggested. He'd put his results into two columns. Success or failure. And yet... His lips curved in a small smile. "Mild to little success does not keep a business running or a sister cared for."

Thunder rumbled outside. Their carriage rattled along the uneven Roman roads that led them farther out of London. "Then... it should be an easy decision," Gillian said softly.

Only, it wasn't.

She removed her hand from his, and he wanted to call it back. Understanding filled her eyes. "You don't want to leave London."

She spoke as one who knew him. But then, she'd always known him better than anyone. "My mother passed some years ago, but my sister...she is here." He made a show of adjusting his makeshift work station. "I'm responsible for her."

"Is she not with your brother Lord Vail?"

His mouth tensed. "And?" he asked tersely.

Gillian, however, slid closer, the only one in the whole damned world who wasn't deterred by those brusque tones. "Is she unhappy living with the baron and his wife?"

"No."

"Is she happy there?"

"She is." In fact, visiting her there and seeing her with Vail and Bridget's children as she took part in family festivities and celebrations, he'd seen that Catriona was happier than he'd ever known her. And mayhap that was why he was unable to relinquish the role he'd assumed these years. Because then it would be a mark that he'd failed her all these years.

A sound of frustration left him. "It's more complicated than... that." *Is it really?* a voice jeered him. Was it truly about Catriona, or his need to find some hint that he'd been able to offer her... something?

"Do you know what I think, Colin? You've created a paradoxical situation."

What was she saying? "I don't..."

"Paradoxical. Ideas that are inconsistent. You've placed yourself in a position where the outcomes compete, and as such, you've paralyzed yourself."

He processed those words. What she was saying was complex. And yet, simple, too. There was a blunt directness to them.

He tried again. "If I leave..." Only, what would happen if he left? Catriona would remain with Vail and Bridget and continue to be as happy as she'd been? Never before had he considered the selfishness in how he viewed Catriona and where she was best suited to live. Mayhap she was best suited to live... precisely where she was.

His mind struggled through a realization that should have come to him years before this moment. One he likely wouldn't have come to had it not been for Gillian.

Gillian laid a hand atop his, and he stared at her delicate fingers covering his larger, work-roughened ones. Two hands so entirely different, just as the pairing of him and Gillian had been since they were children. And yet, at the same time, so wholly right.

"You feel guilty for what happened," she said somberly. "You regret that our friendship saw your sister and your mother cast out."

He didn't deny it because he couldn't. He'd lived only with guilt since the day the mail coach had drawn them away from Cheshire and onto the roughest streets in London.

That was also why he'd committed himself to caring for Catriona. And why he'd accepted the assistance Vail had held out.

His throat tightened, and he shifted his gaze to the top of her pale curls, unable to meet that stare of hers, the piercing one that could pluck out every secret he'd ever had and intended to hold close, making them her own.

"Every time I'm selfish, she has suffered."

His brother's warning hung there, hovering in his mind.

He ruined you once. He'll do it again.

He didn't want you dealing with his daughter when you were children. Do you think he's going to suddenly prove magnanimous towards any relationships between the two of you now that you're grown?

If it was discovered he'd helped Gillian, the marquess could and would see not only Colin ruined, but Catriona. Catriona, who by her birthright and history, was already enough of a social outcast.

But God help him, neither could he abandon Gillian.

Gillian quit the spot on her bench, and shifting the books on his seat over onto hers, she joined him, sitting side by side. "You told me I'm not responsible for my father's actions."

"You're not," he said automatically and then froze, realizing too late what she'd said. His neck went hot. "It's not the same."

"Isn't it? You would blame yourself for the same reasons, Colin." She didn't allow him a word edgewise. "Your friendship with me had you and your family cast out. You insisted it wasn't my fault, but, Colin," she went on, her voice entreating, "if it wasn't my fault, then it couldn't be your fault either. Do you know whose fault it is?" She didn't give him a chance to answer. "It is my father's. He is the one who wronged you. His actions were his. They are his, still."

For so long, there had been only guilt. A need to make wrongs right. To give his sister security when she'd gone without it for so long.

"You are right."

Gillian flashed a smile, the whimsical, ethereal one that marked her as an otherworldly beauty. "I know." She abruptly shifted their discourse. "Now, what of Birmingham?" She was already reaching for his papers.

It was a boldness none, not even his siblings, would have dared considered, let alone attempted.

With Gillian, however, they'd shared... everything. And there was an odd sense of rightness in her expecting she had a right to look at his materials.

"It is bustling. Not quite London, but a serious metropolis of its own."

"And so your partner is suggesting you move to Birmingham because of the size of the city?"

"And the lack of police force there. Yes."

She turned through those pages, evaluating the side-by-side columns of numbers and notes.

"You will certainly save more in your rent and expenses," she noted.

There'd never been anything she couldn't do. As someone who rather detested computations, he had always been awed and baffled by her skill with numbers.

Licking the tip of her finger, she flipped to the next page and stopped. "One hundred and two miles," she murmured.

"Not so very far," he said. And yet, it was. Before, he'd been singularly fixed on being so far away from Catriona and the resulting inability to help should she require it. But he had also felt guilt at shirking his responsibilities, passing them off onto Vail.

Now, that distance represented something more. Space between him and Gillian. For when they parted ways once he delivered her to Francesca's and he continued to Birmingham, they'd go about living their lives. He would continue on with his work as an investigator, just as he'd done for the past seven years. His meeting with Barber; one that had involved Colin solidly thrashing him within an inch of his life and the promise of death, had ensured Lord Barber would never mention Gillian's name. As such, Gillian would one day return and resume her place among Polite Society.

And that idea left him... bereft. The idea of their parting.

Only, the distance between them? It was far greater than miles or carriage rides. It was their past, and her father, and their differences in station.

Gillian's voice cut across the desolation of those thoughts. "You should do it, Colin."

"Hmm?" he asked blankly.

"You've lived so long for others. Even our friendship didn't begin as something you wanted."

He made a sound of protest, but she put a fingertip against his lips, quieting those words.

"You've lived for your sister. But you cannot truly be everything you want to be for everyone else unless you take care of your own dreams first."

"It would be…" *Selfish.* Or that's what he'd told himself, because guilt had consumed him for the better part of his life.

Gillian gave him a long, knowing look.

"There are so many reasons not to do it," he said, his response and his tone weak to his own ears.

"Oh?" Gillian flipped through the folder of information his partner had assembled. "Based on this, you'd face less competition, and yet, given the social makeup of those in Birmingham, you'd still be capable of charging close to the same fees as you do now. And your reduced expenses would allow for greater profit and, thereby, an ability to hire more staff to in turn create your own competing metropolitan police force… of sorts." Gillian looked up. "Do I have all that?"

"I…" Head spinning, he glanced down at the pages she held in her fingers. For, when presented that way, it was completely logical… It only made sense what he needed to do. What he should do. And instead, he, who'd persuaded his partner to quit the security of his runner position, had held the other man back from doing what was best for their business.

"You're… not wrong," he said gruffly, slowly taking the packet O'Toole had put together for him.

He had been wrong. Colin.

Gillian touched his hand again, and he met her direct gaze. "Sometimes it just takes a friend to help one see that which one already knows to be truth." She smiled. "That is what you did for me."

For the first time in longer than he could remember... there was a peace. A sense of rightness devoid of guilt.

Because of her... his friend.

And yet, with her settling in to read her book, he felt an overwhelming sense of regret that *friends* were all they, in fact, were.

CHAPTER 17

The violent storms had wrought havoc upon the countryside, leaving the roads mud-clogged and rutted. What would have otherwise been a twelve-hour journey had only been lengthened.

As such, not even halfway to their destination, they stopped for the night.

Being truthful with herself, Gillian was glad for it.

She was glad for the added time she'd had with Colin. She was glad for the conversations they'd exchanged in the carriage. And the jokes and stories they'd shared.

And her heart was going to break all over again with the loss of him when he finally deposited her with Francesca and Lathan. If the newly married husband and wife she spoke of accepted her in, that was. There'd not even been time to send a note. Why, mayhap they wouldn't allow her to stay with them and she would have to remain with Colin and...

And you are allowing yourself a dream of more time with Colin. Something that isn't to be.

For, of course, Francesca would welcome Gillian. And then Gillian and Colin would part ways.

"Gillian?" he shouted up into the storm, bringing her back to the present.

She gave her head a clearing shake; she'd not allow herself to sour their last moments together with sadness.

Holding an umbrella aloft, Colin helped her down from the carriage, and keeping her hand in his, he guided them quickly down the uneven stones that led to the inn. As she kept pace, sliding and laughing as they went, she could almost believe this was real.

The two of them.

The future she'd wanted.

One that, in her mind, had always included a loving, entirely-devoted-to-her husband, as her sister had managed to find. And Francesca. And Phoebe. And of those women she called friends, all who'd *wished* to find love.

A wave of melancholy chased away her laughter, and as Colin opened the narrow, wooden door, she slipped in ahead of him.

The noisy taproom, filled with tables brimming with patrons, came to a screeching halt as everyone stared at Gillian and Colin…

Before dismissing them and returning once more to their drinks and revelry and discourse.

"It appears busy," Gillian said as a graying woman with a slightly hunched back limped over.

"Ye've got coin?" she called, her voice peaking above the din of the taproom.

"I do," Colin said the moment she stopped before them.

Hands on her hips, the old woman looked them both up and down, her gaze lingering on the pearl fastenings of Gillian's cloak. "Yea, Oi'd say ye do."

"We'll require two rooms," Colin said. Lowering Gillian's bag to the floor, he removed his gloves and stuffed them inside his pocket. "Next to one another."

"Ye some fancy lord, are ye?" The old woman snorted. Putting her hands on her hips, she gave Colin and Gillian another once-over. "This one 'as the look of a lady, though, don't she?"

Colin slid his hand into Gillian's, and their fingers twined so naturally. "She is my wife."

Gillian's heart danced wildly. They played at pretend, and only before an innkeeper they'd never see again after the morrow, and—

"Then sleep with yer wife." The old woman cackled. "Unless yer one of those peculiar lords who can't be bothered to share a bed."

An endearing blush filled Colin's cheeks, and he swiftly drew his hand back. He frowned. "I said—"

"An' Oi said Oi've got one room." Her gaze sharpened on him as she eyed him shrewdly. "Unless ye wantin' me to be kickin' someone out of their accommodations for the noight?" She shrugged. "That'll cost ye."

The lines at the corners of Colin's mouth deepened.

Gillian slipped her palm in his once more and shook her head slightly. She'd not have them responsible for someone being displaced by a greedy innkeeper. Her parents would have thought nothing of putting their comforts above others'. Gillian wouldn't ever let herself be like them in that regard. Or in any regard.

Colin nodded tightly. "Very well. I trust this is sufficient." The moment he passed a small purse into the old woman's hands, she was already going through it.

She grunted. "Follow me." Not waiting to see if they followed, she stomped away.

Gillian and Colin climbed the narrow stairway to reach an even narrower corridor with doorways all but on top of one another. As they were led down the hall, Gillian passed her gaze over the walls, some twenty years or more overdue for a coat of paint. The white plaster was cracked and damp, the musty smell of age overpowering the scent of fire that had filled the taproom.

All the while, she was aware of Colin's stare on her.

"'Ere we are," the woman said, removing an enormous circle of keys. Opening one of the doors, she motioned for them to enter.

Colin went in first and did a sweep of the tiny quarters. The bed, overwhelming the room, was nearly three-quarters of a size smaller than Gillian's own mattress. Aside from a washbasin, a crude-looking armoire, and an unsteady oak nightstand, the room was devoid of furniture or ornamentation.

"Ye can 'ang yer garments on the 'ooks there," the innkeeper said, and Gillian looked at the jagged nails the woman indicated.

"Ye got a problem with it?" she asked when neither Gillian nor Colin spoke.

Forcing a smile to her lips, Gillian swept over. "Not at all,

Mrs. . . . ?"

The innkeeper's white eyebrows came together in a tense, suspicious line. "Miss Pyatt. Never married, Oi did."

"Indeed?"

"Surprised, Yar Highness?"

"Impressed at what you've accomplished, when… opportunities are few for women of all stations."

Surprise rounded the old woman's eyes. "Hmph." And yet, this time with the grunt, there came a slight softening of her tone.

"The accommodations are splendid, and we thank you for allowing us the use of your last and final room." Fetching a coin from her reticule, she pressed it into the old woman's hand. "Thank you for your hospitality, Miss Pyatt."

Miss Pyatt handed a key to Gillian and then limped the few steps back to the doorway. "I'll send ye a dish of stew," she said gruffly. "And a bath. Oi expect ye'll be wantin' a bath."

"Thank you so much. That all sounds divine," Gillian murmured.

Miss Pyatt looked over to Colin.

He immediately removed his damp hat.

All hint of the innkeeper's warmth evaporated. She scowled at Colin. "If this one wants to eat, he can go belowstairs like the others for his meal." With that, she slammed the panel shut behind her.

Gillian's lips pulled in a smile. "I like her."

He laughed; this was his full and boisterous laugh she'd delighted in eliciting from him years and years ago. "You… *like* her?"

"I do," she said defensively. "She is direct and… interesting."

"You charmed her."

"I spoke the truth," she said, unfastening the buttons of her cloak. Gillian hung the article on one of the nails that looked strained from years of too many usages. "I was impressed by her."

"*Indeed?*"

At his incredulity, she turned back to face him. "And why shouldn't she be admired? Because she's suspicious when everything in life has proven that a woman has every reason to be wary?" Hadn't she, the daughter of a marquess, herself learned that lesson just a month earlier? "Miss Pyatt has made her way on her own. She has a thriving business." Frowning, she rested her shoulder against the wall. "She's accomplished far more than most. Certainly far more than me." She added that last afterthought more for herself.

"You do yourself a disservice."

"I'm not on an expedition for compliments, Colin," she said as he shed his cloak and placed it on the hook alongside hers. He'd only ever defended her.

"I never simply say something for the sake of saying it, Gillian. You know that about me."

Yes, that much was true. And yet...

"What is there to be impressed by with my existence? I've had five London Seasons." She lifted her right palm. As she spoke, she proceeded to lower a finger. "I've not traveled." Unlike her friend Phoebe. Phoebe, who even as a young mother had seen the world. "I've not had any responsibility overseeing estates or business affairs." Not as Francesca had done. "I've no great talents in art." As Genevieve did. "I've not involved myself in charitable ventures. And I've no idea what my future holds beyond... *this*." Sinking onto the edge of the mattress, she stared blankly at the clenched fist she'd formed with each of those five deductions. For, when looking at one's life in that very clear way, one was hard-pressed to be anything but forlorn by the state of one's existence.

Sometime tomorrow, or the next day, she would arrive at Francesca's cottage... and... be left with the same question she had today: What happened next?

The wide-planked floorboards groaned as Colin sank to his haunches beside her. She looked at him, and her heart jumped just as it always did when he was near.

"You were a girl who always championed and supported those in need of supporting," he said quietly. "It wasn't just me. It was all the other underprivileged in the village. And that generosity extended to an innkeeper woman whose likely never known a day's kindness from the people who pass through these halls."

She sighed. "You make more of it than there was or is. There's nothing brave in treating people as they ought to be treated, in forming friendships where one would."

"Not to you, perhaps, Gillian. But it was everything to me." His knuckles scraped gently along her jaw, and she edged her gaze up to meet his. "Everything."

As he spoke, his voice deep and husky, she could almost believe that offering. A wistful smile edged her lips up, and she lightly stroked her fingers through his dark curls. "Look at you."

"What about me?"

"Despite life's cruelty…" Nay, that wasn't what it had been. "Despite my father's interference in your life," she made herself say, owing it to Colin to name her father as the criminal he was, "you made a good life for yourself. You traveled to a place that is cold and cruel, and you not only survived, Colin, you thrived," she said, her voice impassioned. "You cared for your sister. You became a successful runner. You own your own business." Even with all that, he'd set out to grow his venture even more.

And then there was… her.

She let her hand fall back to her lap.

Colin straightened and then sat beside her. The lumpy mattress dipped under the addition of his weight. "Even bastard-born, I've had advantages that you haven't. Being born a man in a world where men set the rules, there have been opportunities available to me that aren't the same for women."

No, a woman went from being a daughter to being married, at which point she became… property.

"You refused to let your father or… or the one who wronged you," he went on, "determine your fate. You took ownership of your future, disregarding their worthless opinions and wishes for you. And you have never let your station dictate the relationships you would form or the connections you would have. And *that*, Gillian, is a mark of your strength."

All her life, she'd regretted not being more, lamented not having any great accomplishments. Only for Colin to make her look at herself and her life, and how she'd lived it with no concern for her father's judgment or Society's regard, in a new way. Her heart swelled with so much love for this man.

Why couldn't she have reunited with him before the night of that masquerade?

Why couldn't she have gone to him and rekindled their

relationship before she'd needed to make herself a burden?

How much would be different even now?

And how desperately she wished for it to be different.

His gaze slipped to her mouth.

Of its own volition, her head drifted up as she angled herself so very naturally toward him... and his kiss. The promise of his lips on hers whispered in the air with the same intensity as the lightning poised to strike outside in the violent tempest.

Colin lowered his mouth toward hers a tiniest fraction, the smallest movement sending a lock falling across his brow.

Gillian brushed the strand back.

He was a number of inches taller than her, so her gaze fell in line with his slight Adam's apple. That small knob moved wildly.

Heat burned between them, as volatile and electric as the storm that raged outside.

All she knew was she wanted him... and his kiss and all of his embrace.

She wanted to—

Colin jumped up. "I should leave you to your... to your ablutions," he croaked, and then grabbing his hat from one of those crooked hooks, he jammed it atop his head. "Lock the door behind me."

And with that, he left.

Her cheeks aflame, she remained locked to her spot. Why had he fled?

Because he was a man of honor. Had he been anyone else, she would have easily believed it was disgust with her and her past with Lord Barber. But Colin... he was different. He'd been clear about the desire he felt for her and his fear of being less than honorable toward her.

Gillian stood. Padding across the room, she followed the same path Colin had hastily traveled and leaned her forehead against the drafty panel.

Through the faintest crack, she spied him on the other side.

Gillian squinted, fighting to bring his figure into greater focus. The handle of lit sconces cast the barest of glows upon the corridor. She pressed her eye closer and peered out.

Twisting his hat in his hands, Colin paced back and forth, a quick, unsteady path. Periodically, he stole a glance at the door.

I want him to return. I don't want him to go belowstairs.

She felt closer with him than she did... anyone. Their bond had been forged as children and only just rekindled all these years later. He slowed his steps, and Gillian froze, holding her breath, believing for a moment that he spied her there spying upon him.

She made herself turn the lock.

That slight metallic click penetrated the quiet.

Colin stopped his pacing, and then jamming his hat atop his dark hair once more, he gave the door a final look before heading for the stairway down into the taproom.

The understanding of why he'd remained outside their shared rooms hit her. He'd been waiting until he'd known she'd slid the lock into place. He'd stayed long enough to verify that she was safe.

Gillian turned, resting her back against the panel, and stared over at where her cloak rested alongside his. There should be just one question she was focused on: What happened to her after Colin took her to Francesca's?

Even knowing all her energies and attention should be on that concerning part of her future, she could focus on just one.

How was she going to survive losing Colin Lockhart for a second time?

CHAPTER 18

COLIN HAD FACED ANY NUMBER of daunting tasks in the course of not only his career as a runner, but in the whole of his life.

But this night's task would rival every damned assignment that had come before—sharing a room with Gillian.

Oh, she'd slept in his chambers before, but he'd not been in the same room as her.

There had been distance and a door, and because of those barriers, he'd not had to listen to the rustle of fabric as she turned in her sleep or hear the deep and steady breaths she drew as she slumbered.

Nay, this night… shortly, he'd climb the stairs and enter a room they shared, and he would be tested in ways he'd never been tested before.

Colin reached past the Birmingham folder for the same tankard he'd been drinking from for the better part of an hour and took a long swallow of the heavily watered-down brew. All the while, he eyed the narrow stone stairwell that led—

Someone slammed a pitcher down on his table, sloshing water over the side and into the bowl of stew he'd been served nearly an hour ago.

He looked up.

Miss Pyatt glared back.

"Ye been eyeing that stairway since ye got down 'ere. Ye expectin' company?"

"No." Colin hurriedly closed his folder.

He needn't have worried. The old innkeeper didn't so much as pass a cursory look over his folio… his now slightly damp folio.

She held her pitcher aloft, and he shook his head. "That will not be—"

Miss Pyatt was already refilling his half-empty tankard. "Of course it's necessary. Oi don't get paid if yer just sittin' there starin' at my stairwell."

"Fair point," he muttered.

"Of course it is. I'm a clever businesswoman."

The innkeeper kept a full inn and saw that plates were out and glasses full, maximizing profit with every moment her patrons were filling up the hall.

"Yes, my…" *My wife.* They were two words that should have horrified him to even utter in pretend. He'd resolved to never have any mistress other than his work. And yet, a memory of his carriage ride that day with Gillian whispered forward. Gillian looking over his work with him and sharing her opinion and making him think of Birmingham when he'd been determined to flat-out reject the possibility of a move. There'd been something so very… right in that exchange.

He felt Miss Pyatt's piercing stare, and he cleared those nonsensical thoughts.

"My wife spoke highly of your accomplishments."

"Yer wife," she muttered. Hiking up her skirts, she sat in the chair across from him. "Ye ain't married to that girl."

Colin went absolutely motionless. "Of course I am," he said, the belated assurance earning a snort from Miss Pyatt loud enough to rise above the taproom din.

"Elopin'?" she asked instead. "Some advice?" She didn't wait for his invitation. "Get the girl to Gretna Green before she realizes she can do better than a man hiding in my taproom and making moon-eyes at my stairs." With that, Miss Pyatt struggled to stand.

Automatically coming to his feet, he extended a hand to help her.

Miss Pyatt cackled. "Go on with yerself. Helpin' me." Even as she groused, a blush filled her gaunt, wrinkled cheeks. "Mayhap ye ain't so very bad after all." She rapped his knuckles sharply and scowled. "But Oi can take care of meself, yer lordship." With that, she gathered up her pitcher.

"I'm not..." *A nobleman.* She'd already limped onward to fill the tankards at the next table of patrons.

The thing of it was, how very much would have been different in his life had he been born the legitimate child of his ducal father? His and Gillian's relationship would have never been forbidden. And what would that have meant for them?

His face pulled with self-disgust, and he made himself head for his rooms. He wasn't a man to pine over "what could've's." And he certainly wasn't one to make *moon-eyes*. By God, he was Colin Lockhart. The damned finest runner on any end of London and now a self-made businessman in his own right. Still ruthless. And he was certainly not a man who should be afraid to share a room with a sleeping woman.

He had restraint.

He had self-control.

And honor.

With those reminders peppering his brain, he fished the key out and let himself into his and Gillian's temporary rooms. The panel groaned as he made his way in and then squealed all the louder as he closed and locked it behind him.

Miss Pyatt, in addition to sending the wood tub that now filled the corner of the room, had sent someone to tend a fire. The meager blaze cast the barest hint of warmth and light over the dank chambers.

Leaning against the wood panel, Colin wrestled one of his boots off. He carefully lowered the article to the floor. As he removed the other, his gaze strayed over to where Gillian rested in the middle of that tiny bed. She lay much the same way she had when they'd snuck out to watch for shooting stars—flat on her back, with her hands folded atop her stomach. And he proved weaker than he'd convinced himself he was on his way up, for he could not force his eyes from her. Just as he could not force back those happiest of memories, the ones he'd made himself forget, all in the name of self-preservation. Because it had been easier not thinking on the happier times than it had been missing those moments spent with her.

Tiptoeing across the room, he hung up his hat, and then shrugging out of his jacket, he carried it to the last sliver of space available in the room—beside her bed.

Calling on every last sliver of restraint he'd arrogantly lauded himself for on the way up, he forcibly kept his gaze from straying to Gillian's sleeping form. Tossing his jacket down, he lowered himself to the floor and lay there. The cold and slightly damp floor penetrated his wool shirt, the misery a welcome distraction from the thought that if he stretched his arm out, he could actually touch her.

The mattress squeaked loudly as Gillian rolled onto her side.

Resting her head on her palm, she stared down at him. "You are not sleeping down there."

With a black curse that would have shocked any other lady, Colin shot upright. "Bloody hell, Gillian. What are you doing?"

"Arguing with you."

"Yes, yes, I see that. I meant before. Why aren't you sleeping?"

"I cannot sleep," she confessed, and sitting up, she drew her knees up close to her chest and folded her arms around them. "And it is a good thing I could not, or I'd have otherwise failed to see that you intended to sleep down there."

"And just where do you expect I should sleep?" It was the absolute wrong question to ask. He knew it as soon as it left his mouth. Knew it because this was Gillian.

"Why, with me, of course."

Of course.

His pulse hammered in his ears and in parts of his body he didn't know a pulse could pound.

"We can talk just like we used to," she prattled on, wholly oblivious to the torment she'd unleashed within him, and all at the imagining of his joining her on that mattress. "Or tell riddles or play word games or…"

If he were capable of laughing through the torment of this moment, he would have managed it just then at the idea of joining her in any game. His brow dipped. That was, any game that wasn't sexual in nature.

"Or we can just talk about Birmingham," she was saying. She flipped onto her side again. "Why, it isn't as though we've not slept alongside each other before," she said, her conversational tones at odds with the surge of lust as he merely thought of climbing onto that mattress.

Colin fought off all those wicked, dangerous musings, ones that included her and him, their limbs entangled, their mouths on each other. Everywhere.

"This is different," he said between clenched teeth.

The mattress squeaked as she leaned closer. "How so?" she asked with more hesitancy than he ever remembered from her.

He gulped. An audible, damning-to-his-own-ears sound that brought her leaning over the side of the bed to peer at him. And his already razor-fine thread of control snapped. "Because, damn it, we aren't children anymore, Gillian," he exploded.

There were several beats of silence, made all the damningly more tense by the echo of his sharp words hovering in the air still.

"I... see." The bed squealed once more as she fell back into the mattress.

Good, let her believe she saw. Letting her to whatever conclusion she'd arrived at was far safer than acknowledging his weakness—nay, his desire—for her. Damn him for not being strong enough to let her see whatever lie it was that she thought she saw... because he could not hurt her. Just as he couldn't have lies between them.

Bloody hell.

"I want you," he said hoarsely. "I want you in ways that I have no place wanting you."

Not when tomorrow he'd say goodbye to her forever.

～

Lying back, she stared overhead at a wide watermark dripping rain in the corner.

He wanted her.

"Oh." And if she were more experienced, more worldly, she would have said something other than that utterance.

Gillian's belly danced wildly. There was a headiness to that realization. That was why he'd rushed off and why he craved distance whenever she was near.

Rolling onto her side, she faced him.

His eyes were squeezed shut, and he lay so motionless that she could have convinced herself that she'd merely imagined the words he'd spoken.

"Colin," she said softly.

He looked Gillian's way.

"I want you, too." And there was a beautiful peace in owning that truth; there wasn't shame.

Sitting up so that his back rested against the bed, Colin covered his face with his hands. "Gillian." Her name emerged as an entreaty.

Gillian swung her legs over the side of the bed and sank onto the floor to join him. "*You* are the one who said I am entitled to my choices, Colin. Why can you not be... one of my choices?"

He dropped his palms and angled himself so that he could hold her gaze squarely. "Because you'll regret it," he said flatly.

Gillian frowned. "I won't, Colin." The only regret she'd have was when they parted ways, that there couldn't have ever been more between them. She caught one of his hands in hers and drew it close to her chest. "I was robbed before of the most important decision a woman might make, but you are who I choose now."

She felt him wavering. She saw it in his eyes. And she heard it in the next words he spoke.

"I can't... give you more. I have my work. I have my new business, one that will likely be moving to Birmingham."

There was no place for a wife in his life. His meaning was clear.

"I know those things, Colin. I'm not asking you for anything more... than one night. Then we will part ways and..." *And I will yearn for you still.*

"And we'll return to being friends?"

She dropped her chin atop her knees. No, there could be no doubting that whatever came of this night, nothing would be the same between them. *Ever.*

But when presented with the possibility of having none of him or just this moment with which to hold on to forever, she would choose the latter.

Gillian sat upright. "There won't be any regrets, Colin. I'm a woman who knows what I want."

A pained-sounding laugh spilled from his lips, and his mirth sent their shoulders brushing against each other. "Yes, you always have been, Gillian."

And then cupping her about the nape, he lowered his mouth to hers, and just as there'd been every time he'd embraced her, there came the instant sparks, electrifying and shocking for the wonder of them. They sent a thrill shooting through her, to her belly and lower. And she kissed him back, opening her mouth for him and allowing him to sweep his tongue inside.

Coming up onto her knees, she leaned into him and his kiss, clutching the fabric of his wool shirt and dragging herself closer.

Colin settled his hands around her waist. His fingers drifted lower, and he sank them into her hips, guiding her up and onto his lap.

All the while, he continued the sweet sweep of his tongue within the cavern of her mouth in a kiss that was primal and raw, a kiss that should terrify, but its overwhelming intensity pulled her deeper and deeper into the web of arousal he spun around her senses.

She shifted on his lap so she could better meet each hungry slash of his tongue against hers. Her night skirts came up, rucking about her waist, and the cool air slapped at her heated skin.

There were no words, just the rasps of their breath, coming unsteady and off tempo. And the slick glide of their tongues meeting. Those forbidden sounds only further fueled her desire. The ache between her legs throbbed, and her hips moved reflexively in a bid to ease the pressure there.

Colin panted.

Or was that her own ragged breaths that she released within his mouth?

Everything was mixed up in this moment. Everything within her had been reduced to simply feeling, shattering all ability to sort and reason.

Stretching her legs so that she straddled his lap, she pressed herself against him. Over and over.

To Hold a Lady's Secret

Colin's mouth shifted course, and he dragged a trail of kisses along her jaw. "Have you changed your mind?" he asked between kisses, his voice rough and raspy, and the evidence of his desire caused a visceral reaction within her.

"Never."

That was all he needed.

Colin drew her nightshift up past her shoulders, tossing the article aside and baring her fully to the night air… and his ministrations. Cupping her breasts, he filled his palms, weighing those mounds in his hands.

Her breath hitched as he stroked and teased that flesh. Bringing her breasts together, he raised them up and—

Gillian's eyes slid closed, and a moan got stuck in her throat as he teased first one tip and then the other pebbled peak. The day's growth of beard upon his cheeks scraped flesh sensitized by his every caress. He drew the tip deep within his mouth… and suckled.

Gillian cried out, her fingers tightening reflexively in his hair. She anchored him close, keeping his mouth on her, determined that he should never, ever stop.

And he didn't.

He flicked his tongue over that peak. Again. And again.

Gillian pumped her hips against him, her pace growing increasingly frantic as every sensation tunneled at just one place, the growing heat at the apex of her thighs.

Tugging his shirt from the waistband of his trousers, she pulled it up and wrestled it from him so that she could feel his flesh against hers, needing to feel the heat of his skin, every sinew, every muscle gloriously defined. He was a masculine masterpiece of power and strength, slicked with the sweat that glistened upon that hardened canvas.

Gillian glided her fingers over the light matting of dark hair that covered his chest.

He shuddered, and she lifted her head, searching for an indication that she'd hurt him. She detected the same sentiment reflected back in his eyes, the one where pleasure blurred with the kind of pain that one was happy to surrender oneself to.

Then his midnight lashes dipped, hooding his gaze a moment before his mouth was on hers. He slid a hand between their bodies, and—a hiss burst from her lips, that sound swallowed by his mouth as he palmed her center. Her hips shot forward as she struggled to get closer to that illicit touch.

And then he was stroking her, gliding first one finger through moist curls, finding that most sensitive place within her, a place of pure, delicious sensation.

Throwing her head back, Gillian cried out.

She dimly registered him scooping her up in his arms and depositing her on the mattress. It dipped and sagged as he came down over her, framing her between his arms. Sweat slicked their bodies, his and hers, melded together. And where there'd been cold before, there was a conflagration he'd set ablaze within her, consuming her from the inside out.

"So… beautiful." His voice came terse and broken and harsh, as if desire had dissolved his speech. And then he tried again. "You are so beautiful." Colin swooped his head down to worship the tip of her right breast, laving that peak, suckling. Teasing. Tasting. All the while, his fingers continued their slow glide within her.

Gillian bit down on her lower lip hard enough that she tasted the metallic tinge of blood.

Sweat dripped down the side of her temple as she lunged her hips up, desperately seeking… more. "Colin," she panted. Her legs fell open, and he sank between her thighs, knowing implicitly what she begged for.

His length, long and hot like steel kissed by the sun, nudged past her damp curls.

Gillian's breath came fast, heavy respirations that came as hard as the pulse beating a rhythm in her ears, and her body leaned into what he held out. The promise of… more.

Colin slipped deep inside, sliding himself into her sheath, and her eyes slid shut. "Mm. Mm." There was no shame. There was only this glorious sense of joy and control… of what she wanted. Of this moment.

And that, at last, it was with the man whom she'd always yearned for.

Taking her mouth in another kiss, Colin eased deeper into her. The glide slow and blissful and agonizing all at the same time. Until… he filled her. His enormous length throbbed against the walls of her womanhood. He eased out, inch by aching inch, the pace he set teasing. Torturing.

Then he began to move. Faster. With a growing intensity that pulled a keening cry from her lips that climbed to the rafters and spilled around the room, a heady, erotic echo of her desire.

Dropping his brow to hers, Colin angled his body closer, holding her gaze as he lunged… and withdrew. Gillian tightened her hold about him and lifted her hips in time to his every move.

Moaning, she met his powerful thrusts. Taking him. All of him. Until there was no sense of where he began and she ended, and it was a union she craved from her soul to the place that throbbed between her legs.

Heat pooled and sat there at her center, each nerve, each sensation so sharp, so acute.

Their movements grew more frantic as the pressure built inside. One that pulled her to a place she both feared and felt she would die if she didn't allow herself to go to. And then the decision was no longer hers.

Colin thrust home, and she shattered in a blindingly beautiful climax of light and color. Through her release, she screamed his name over and over again.

And still, he continued to fill her.

His entire body tensed in her arms, and he threw his head back and roared, a primal shout that filled the room and likely the whole tiny inn. Drawing out, Colin poured his release onto her belly in glistening rivulets and then collapsed, catching himself on his elbows to keep from crushing her.

They clung to each other. She wrapped her arms about him and pressed her cheek against the wall of his chest. Under her ear, his heart thumped a wild beat in time to her own.

And folded within the shelter of his arms, she finally admitted she'd lied to herself—one night with Colin Lockhart would never be enough.

CHAPTER 19

HE SHOULD HAVE LEFT SEVEN hours ago.

No, *they* should have left seven hours ago.

The plan had been to arise before the sun and begin the journey onward to Francesca's so that he could, in turn, make his way to Birmingham.

And yet, she'd been sleeping.

And she'd been so endearing in that sleep. Snoring. For all the ways in which they'd known each other and for as long as they had, he'd not known she snored. And while she'd slept, he'd sat at the edge of the bed, staring on and wondering what else did he not know about Gillian. What other little intricacies made her *her*? And then, there'd been the yearning to discover every last one.

That was what had managed to pull him from her side and send him fleeing to the now-empty taproom, where he'd been sitting ever since.

Miss Pyatt moved throughout the room, running a rag over the tables while a young boy cleaned the bar.

"Something wrong with yer meal, prince?"

Her head was bent over her task, so it took a moment to register the innkeeper's words were for him.

He smiled. Between last evening's stew and the morning meal, the fare had proven… surprisingly hearty and tasteful. "Not at all. It is quite delicious, thank you." And to prove as much, he reached for a large, crusty piece of bread and took a bite.

Grunting, Miss Pyatt tossed her cloth down and headed toward her kitchens, leaving Colin alone with his thoughts.

Nay, he'd not been focusing on his meal. He'd been preoccupied with thoughts of Gillian. More specifically...

Letting her go.

Losing her all over again.

Unlike before, when they parted ways this time, there would be an actual goodbye between them, that which they'd been denied as children.

Closure. There'd be closure.

But it wouldn't be enough.

He stared blankly down at the partially eaten piece of bread on his crude metal plate.

As a child, the memory of her had sustained him when he'd been out in London picking pockets to feed his family. Until the memory of her had been harder to live with, and he'd forced aside all thoughts of Gillian Farendale. It had been nearly impossible then.

But now?

This time, there would be no forgetting her, a woman so resilient that she'd demanded an audience at his offices and enlisted his help. A woman who'd been wronged, but who refused to allow herself to be anyone's victim. A woman who'd come alive as she had in his arms just hours a—

"What are ye doin' 'ere?"

He glanced up.

Miss Pyatt tossed a plate down next to his.

"I don't..." He shook his head.

She nudged her chin, and he followed that gesture toward the stairs.

Not so very long ago, he would have ordered the old woman gone. He would have kept his head buried in whatever assignment he'd been working on and would have failed to see Miss Pyatt or anyone. Gillian had opened his eyes to how singularly focused he'd been, at the expense of all personal connections with all, including his own family.

Uninvited, Miss Pyatt pulled out the same uneven chair she'd occupied across from him last evening and seated herself. Colin found himself unexpectedly grateful for the diversion from those thoughts.

"Is there somewhere else I should be?"

"Shouldn't you be on to Gretna Green?" Miss Pyatt laughed as though she'd told the grandest jest.

And then he recalled his and Gillian's ruse. Their pretend marriage. The innkeeper's assumption that they were young lovers on their way to Gretna Green. To acknowledge her question and give an answer, however, would confirm the lie. And even as the clever innkeeper had deduced there was more to his and Gillian's story, he was unwilling to confide anything.

Colin took a bite of his bread. "I told you. We're married."

She cackled. "Aye. Me, too." Miss Pyatt laughed all the harder. When her mirth abated, she dashed the tears from her cheeks. "That one sleeps soundly."

His gaze drifted toward the stairwell to where she slept. Yes, she did. And she snored. She did that, too. And she snorted when she laughed. And…

A pressure gripped his chest, and to give his fingers something to do, he grabbed for the tankard of water and drank.

"The plate is for 'er. Feed 'er and get 'er on 'er way," the old woman said gruffly and then shoved to her feet. "Unless she's changed 'er mind and left while ye're keeping me company down here."

He frowned. It was preposterous. The idea that Gillian would continue on without him, and yet—

Colin jumped up, and collecting his books, he stuffed them into his satchel, swung it over his arm, and then gathered the plate of bread and sausage. "Many thanks to you, Miss Pyatt," he said.

The old woman blushed and waved off his gratitude. "Get going, will ye." Collecting a rag from her pocket, she proceeded to clean Colin's table.

Quickening his stride, he made his way toward his rooms—toward Gillian. Ducking at the low overhang at the top of the stairwell, he collected his key and quietly let himself in.

He immediately froze. He'd believed she still slept. And he hadn't thought about what he would say to her now, following their night of lovemaking. And now before their parting. At some point, Gillian had awakened and changed into a casual yellow day dress.

"Good morning, Colin," she said softly, running a brush through those ethereal blonde tresses that were more a luminescent white than golden, strands that held him transfixed. And last night came rushing back, the feel of those curls as they'd glided through his fingers. She brought that brush to a slow stop and stared questioningly back.

Just as she'd always been, Gillian proved steady. Where Colin? He remained shaken from the night they'd spent together… and their eventual parting today.

A cinch squeezed his chest, and he fought to get air into his lungs and out so that he might breathe.

Gillian's thin, perfectly formed eyebrows dipped, a silent question there.

Feeling color flood his cheeks, he hurried to shut the door behind him. "Forgive me." His voice emerged an octave higher, and feeling like an uncertain boy all over again, he cleared his throat. "I should have knocked." He stood with her dish in his hands. "I… brought you this. Food. It is food." He looked over his offering, even though he already knew what the plate contained, and said anyway, "Bread… and sausage." *Stop it. Of course she can see that it is food.* "Miss Pyatt did. Not that she brought it. Rather, she made it and asked that *I* bring it."

"I—"

"Not that I wouldn't have thought to bring you a meal." *My God, I'm rambling.* He made himself stop. Or he tried to. "I would have. Eventually. That is, I eventually would have had a plate readied and brought up. I just assumed you were…" *Stop.* He firmed his lips and held the dish out. "I should set it down." Hurrying over to the little nightstand, he set her breakfast there.

The plate touched the table with a little clink and wobbled ever so slightly before coming to a stop.

Colin and Gillian stood there.

Silent.

Neither speaking.

Just as he'd predicted, as he'd feared, the unthinkable had happened. Last night had changed… them.

What did it say that, even so, he still would never trade those hours in her arms?

"It is only different if we allow it to be, Colin," she said in gentling tones that managed to erase that worry.

"I don't want it to be different. Us," he amended. "I don't want us to be different."

As she settled onto the heavily wrinkled and tousled sheets, she reached for the bread and took a sturdy bite. Not one of those mincing bites his mother had insisted ladies and women take. The ones Catriona still did. But an unapologetic pull that reminded him all over again of why he loved her.

Colin's every muscle went absolutely stock-still.

Love?

What… was that idea even? Of course he loved her. He always had. His mind shied away from anything more. After all, it was only about the fact that he didn't want to lose her.

And why do you have to? a voice whispered.

As she'd pointed out, why could they not remain… friends?

That steadied him. For when he thought of Gillian in that light and of their relationship going forward, it presented a future with them together… in some way.

Will that be enough?

A heavy knock sounded at the door, a sturdier, more determined one than would belong to Miss Pyatt. A knock that shattered the fantastical musings he'd no place having.

Silently motioning Gillian to the armoire, Colin made his way across the small room and reached for the lock—

Too late.

The door exploded open, and a figure filled the doorway. An unfamiliar figure, one that was decidedly not the marquess or Lord Barber or anyone else whom Colin recognized. Though he was dusty, his luxuriant garments wrinkled and faintly smelling of horseflesh, there could be no doubting two things. One, the intruder was of some influence. And two, he'd ridden a distance.

The stranger shoved the door shut with the heel of his boot, the panel closing with a soft click more ominous than had he slammed that oak slab.

Colin reached slowly for the pistol under his jacket, keeping his fingers close to the handle. There was something... familiar about the man, and because of that, plenty of reason for Colin to be wary.

"May I help you?" he asked coolly.

Ignoring that query, the man passed a shrewd gaze over the tight chambers before lingering on the silver-handled brush that rested amidst the rumpled bed.

The gentleman growled. "Where. Is. She?" he seethed in flawlessly clipped tones layered with steel and ice, and... the promise of death.

Colin, however, had faced down men taller, bulkier, and more evil than the stranger before him. He opened his mouth to tell the bastard where he could go with his high-handed intrusion.

But there came the rapid flurry of footfalls and the rustle of skirts as Gillian surged past him and hurled herself into the arms of the gentleman. "*Cedric!*"

"Gillian," the other man said gruffly, folding her into his arms.

Cedric.

The Marquess of St. Albans.

The brother-in-law.

Also... Colin's half-brother. He'd spent his earliest years resenting the Duke of Ravenscourt's legitimate son for having the security and comfort that Colin had only ever dared to dream of. Now, as the other man spoke to Gillian with a tangible warmth and concern, Colin was made to see him in a new light.

"Is Genevieve—?"

"She is well," the marquess interjected. "She is confined to her bed and still carrying the babe."

That was why she'd not gone to her sister. She'd not wished to be a burden upon the expectant mother.

While he spoke over the top of Gillian's head, the marquess glared darkly at Colin.

It had been so easy for Colin to hate the man. He'd been a rake who should have been looking after Gillian. He hadn't before, but he *was* here now. He'd come for her, which was not the mark of a heartless cad, but rather the mark of one who cared. Nor could there be any doubting that the man now speaking in hushed tones that Colin strained to hear did, in fact, care.

Colin fell back and watched the exchange between the pair, taking in the gentleman's instantly softening features and the worry and the relief in the other man's eyes as he spoke in somber tones. Periodically, Gillian nodded or shook her head.

The moment she'd shown up at his office, the one question—the *only* question—he'd been concerned with was whether there was someone else who could help her. That was, anyone other than him. Because there'd been Colin's work and Birmingham and his sister.

Only, now there *was* someone else, and a keen regret pricked sharp. He didn't want to relinquish her over to this man. Or… any man.

"What are you doing here?" Gillian asked.

"Rescuing you," the marquess said, revealing how little he knew his sister-in-law.

Gillian Farendale would only ever do her own saving.

"I received word that you were in trouble and came immediately." Gillian's brother-in-law leveled another menacing look at Colin.

Gillian followed that stare and frowned. Quitting the marquess's side, she moved to join Colin, placing herself side by side with him, that loyalty, that support so very reminiscent of how she'd defended him years and years ago.

"This is my friend," Gillian said with a slight reproach there. "Colin."

Shrewd eyes landed on Colin once more, assessing ones that pierced and probed, and even as Colin kept his features neutral, he suspected those eyes saw entirely too much. "Your *friend*?"

The other man's gaze turned remarkably conciliatory. "I owe you a debt of gratitude." Lord St. Albans extended a hand.

I don't want your damned thanks. It had only ever been about her. Even back when he'd brought himself around to agreeing to help with the thought that he was paying a debt, deep down in a place he could finally bring himself to acknowledge, it had always been about Gillian.

The marquess's eyebrows came together as a question puckered the place between them.

Colin made himself shake the other man's hand.

"How did you know where to find us?"

Gillian's question brought the marquess's focus back her way. "Lord Chilton paid me a visit and expressed his concern, for both you and Mr. Lockhart. I, of course, came as soon as I heard."

Colin's body tensed. Vail had taken it upon himself to enlist the support of Gillian's brother-in-law. Nor, after his meeting with Vail, could there be any doubting the reason for that interference—he'd worried about Colin's involvement with Gillian's father.

And yet, that had not been Vail's place. The decision had belonged only to Colin. It didn't matter that Colin had initially seen her and her request as a burden. It mattered that he had committed to assisting her and had intended to do so…

"We should leave," Lord St. Albans said to Gillian. "Why don't you take a moment to gather up your things?"

Gillian slid a glance over Colin's way. Her eyes were stricken. "Of course."

Colin's muscles locked. Every sinew froze. Every tendon coiled. And he hurt. All over. In ways he'd never hurt before. Even as it made sense that she'd go on with her brother-in-law. Even as logic, that thing which had driven Colin all these years, said she should go.

I'm not ready.

In his mind, there'd been the remainder of their journey with which to make peace with their parting. With which to say goodbye. It wasn't to have been rushed like this, with Gillian fluttering about the room, gathering her things, and tossing them into her valise.

To hide the faint shaking of his hands, Colin clasped them at his back and stood there. Gillian's brother-in-law was equally silent as she worked.

And then she was done.

The marquess hurried the few steps to relieve Gillian of her burden. The other man was capable of movement when Colin was singularly incapable of anything but thinking one thought. *She is leaving.*

The pressure built in Colin's chest.

Lord St. Albans headed for the door before seeming to realize that Gillian hovered there still.

"Colin," she began softly.

"Don't," he cut her off.

"I didn't say anything."

He let his arms fall to his sides. "You were going to thank me."

A sad little smile played upon those pale pink lips. "You know me too well."

They knew each other.

His throat moved quickly, making it hard to form words. He forced them out anyway, and they emerged hoarsened and rough. "I am"—*going to miss you so damned much*—"honored that you came to me, and…" *I don't want you to go.* There was a question in her eyes. "And it is I who must thank you for opening my eyes to how singularly focused I've been and all I've failed to see."

His gaze drifted sideways, away from her. And yet, what she'd revealed about how he'd lived his life also made it so that when she took her leave, his emotions would be split wide open, forcing him to feel loss all over again. "Be happy, Gillian."

Tears glimmered in her eyes, darkening her irises. "You, as well."

They both lingered there…

Lord St. Albans cleared his throat, effectively breaking the moment.

Gillian hurried over to join her brother-in-law.

The marquess opened the door, waiting for Gillian, and then with one last look over her shoulder for Colin, she was gone.

Colin didn't move. His gaze locked on the wood panel, he didn't so much as blink.

She is gone.

He made himself repeat those three words in his head, in every way and with all manner of inflection. Believing that, in acknowledging it, there'd be an easing of this crushing pain.

There was his work. There was Birmingham and his new firm, and those endeavors would consume him. They'd distract him

To Hold a Lady's Secret

and refocus him on where his efforts needed to be—his failing business.

Only, telling himself all those things didn't make him believe any of it.

His eyes slid shut.

I miss her already.

This time, there would be no forgetting her. There'd be no erasing the time they'd shared together.

Footsteps came from the hall, soft and quiet. Colin's eyes flew open, and he was already across the room and had the door opened.

"Oh."

Miss Pyatt flashed a mocking grin. "Expecting someone else, were ye?"

"No," he said, his voice as hollow as the place in his chest where his heart beat. Just hoping. He'd been hoping to see her.

"Ye let her get away, did ye?" A sound of disgust left Miss Pyatt. "Oi knew if ye dinna rush her out of 'ere, ye'd lose her, an' 'ere we are."

Here we are…

He and Miss Pyatt… and no Gillian.

Miss Pyatt, who'd sense enough after just one meeting to know the gift Colin had and that he should hold on to it with everything. Nay, hold on to her.

And why couldn't he?

Thunder rumbled in the distance.

His pulse stopped and then hammered away at a frantic pace.

Why *couldn't* there be a future for him and Gillian?

All these years, he'd been afraid of losing. Of being hurt. She'd helped him see that he could have more than just his work. He'd worked so very hard to erect protective walls to keep himself from hurting, but keeping her out hadn't eased the pain of losing her. It made the agony only more acute.

Yanking a purse from inside his jacket, he pressed into the old innkeeper's wrinkled hand. "Thank you," he said and took off running past her.

"Took ye long enough, it did," she called, her droll reply chasing after him.

Colin took the stairs quickly.

Yes, it had taken him long enough… nearly thirteen years.

Now, there was the matter of convincing the lady that she wanted a future with him in it.

CHAPTER 20

It was done.

Settled.

In ways she'd not anticipated, but in ways that would see her secure.

As such, there should be only an overwhelming sense of relief and not this… this… great chasm of sadness that had swelled within her chest and invaded every corner of her heart and being since she'd boarded Cedric's carriage and started onward to his country estate.

Gillian stared at three trails of raindrops streaking a path down the windowpane, those crystal trails like tears upon the glass.

The tempest she and Colin had set out in had lessened, with the sky still determined to hold on to its misery.

And it perfectly suited her. She touched a finger to one fat, oval drop as it trickled an uneven path from the middle of the glass downward, zigzagging until it was lost in the seam of the window.

She missed him.

She'd spent years aching to have him back in her life. And to have Colin back only to lose him all over again?

"Why did you not come to us?" Cedric spoke his first words since they'd set out. "Surely you know you can always come to me and Genevieve," he said gently and without recrimination.

Gillian made herself look away from the pastoral scene out

her window. "I… do not doubt you would have moved heaven and earth had I asked it." They would have, even with Genevieve struggling to carry another babe, put Gillian first. "I could never have let myself be that burden." Not willingly. Ultimately, the decision had been taken from her. And then, as she could finally be honest with herself, there had been the simple truth: She'd wanted it to be Colin. She knew that now. In the face of her assault, a heinous act she'd no recollection of, she'd wished to share the aftermath with someone she'd been closer with. A friend who'd never passed judgment and whose relationship she'd missed so very much. Her teeth caught the inside of her cheek as another dose of pain, fresh and sharp still, lashed away at her heart.

Cedric shifted seats, joining her on the bench. "You are *never* a burden," he said in insistent tones. "You are a sister to me." Grief twisted his features. "One that I failed."

She stilled as those four words confirmed what she hadn't even wanted to consider: He knew.

"You found out," she whispered.

Cedric's features were ravaged. "I… received word from a former friend that you may have been in attendance. I… chose to dismiss it as gossip, because…" His voice trailed off.

Nor did he need to finish that statement. He'd been unable to believe she would have attended such an event. On the heels of that came the horrifying whisperings at the back of her mind: How much did he know? Gillian shied away from that question. Unable to meet those guilt-filled eyes, she stared down at her lap. "The masquerade wasn't nearly as glamorous or as grand as I thought it would be."

"Oh, God." Cedric dragged a hand through his damp and tousled hair. "I should have come when I learned."

"No. You shouldn't have." He had two babes and a wife who was expecting their third child. "I'm not your responsibility."

"It is not about seeing you as a responsibility. I love you as a sister, and in your thinking that your only course was to go to a stranger and not me? Then I have *failed* you."

A stranger. That was how he'd describe Colin, and with that, how easily Cedric should diminish Colin's role, but then, her brother-in-law didn't know the depth and length of her friendship with Colin. He didn't know the love she'd carried for Colin all these years.

Gillian's shoulders came back. "He is not a stranger. He is a friend who also happens to be your brother."

Cedric's jaw went slack. "*Whaaat?*" That query emerged strangled.

She gentled her tones. "He is one of your father's illegitimate children, Cedric. And he was my friend for many, many years." Before her father had gone and ripped up the lives of Colin and his family… and her friendship with him.

"I… didn't know." As if she'd landed a blow to his midsection, Cedric slumped, sinking back on the bench.

He'd not known Colin nor the baron were his brothers? "You *should* have," she said. The world should look so unfavorably upon Colin, and all because he'd been born outside of wedlock to a duke who refused to acknowledge his existence. Where Cedric had failed to see Colin, Colin had forged bonds with his half siblings, forming meaningful connections that didn't take into consideration the type of blood in their veins.

"Yes. Yes. I…" Her brother-in-law's face buckled once more, and he looked away. "I… should have known as much. About his identity. About… all of them."

Only, he misunderstood her.

Gillian angled herself on the bench so she could look squarely at her brother-in-law. "You are not responsible for your father's failings, Cedric. I merely meant to suggest that you take time to find your siblings and know them, because of the people they are. People like Colin, who is honorable and good and devoted to helping anyone." Including Gillian, when any other man would have been bent on revenge and filled with resentment because of what her father had done. Tears filled her eyes, blurring her vision. "You would adore him." Nay… "You would love him."

She felt Cedric's stare upon her.

"Oh… God," he whispered, his words a prayer.

Gillian shook her head. "Please, don't—"

Only, he'd not oblige.

"You *love* him."

She pressed her eyes closed.

In the end, she was saved from answering. Or mayhap *saved* was not the correct word.

The carriage lurched, the back wheels sliding back and forth.

Gillian went flying against the window, and she gripped the side of the bench to steady herself.

"What in hell?" Cedric bellowed.

"Highwaymen," the driver shouted back before the conveyance skidded to a long, slow stop. It rocked once and then settled.

Highwaymen?

"Not a team of them, my lord. Just one."

Cedric had already opened the door and jumped out. "Oh, bloody hell. Lower your gun, Josiah," her brother-in-law shouted up to the driver, before turning his attention out once more. "What is the meaning of this?" he thundered.

Gillian followed quickly behind him.

Cursing, Cedric immediately turned back. "Gillian, get inside."

At some point, the rain had stopped, and the sun peaked out, casting the softest light upon the mud-slicked roads... and the figure several paces away, now dismounting from his horse.

Her heart forgot its sole job was to beat.

"Colin," she whispered and stepped around her brother-in-law.

His midnight tresses were wet from the rain. His garments, equally damp, clung to his contoured frame. As he walked, the wind caught his dark hair and blew at those strands.

"My God, man, were you attempting to get us killed?"

"Forgive me," Colin called out, his voice a booming echo across the barren countryside. As his long-legged stride ate away the distance, however, his focus was reserved solely for Gillian.

"Gillian," her brother-in-law murmured.

"I want to speak to him," she said, following Colin's approach. She *needed* to speak to him. For she would selfishly steal whatever moments there were to be had with Colin.

Cedric hesitated and then backed away to the side of the road, close enough at hand should she need him, but far enough to allow her a hint of privacy.

At last, Colin reached her.

Gillian drank in the sight of him, from his beautifully chiseled cheeks to his slightly too-proud jawline, wanting to preserve this moment.

"It occurred to me after you left that you'd forgotten something."

His words penetrated the joy of his unexpected appearance. And that same organ that had filled with a buoyant lightness at his arrival sank to her toes. That was why he was here. She'd left something behind.

"I… did?" Nothing that she'd carried from London with him would have mattered nearly so much.

"When you came to me, you only presented one set of terms to our arrangement."

An errant wind tugged at her skirts and sent them slapping against Colin's legs. She shook her head in confusion. "I don't understand."

"You referenced the agreement we'd struck, to wed at twenty-three years of age. It wasn't until you left that I recalled." Removing a sheet from inside his cloak, he held it out, and her gaze flew to that aged parchment, the scrawl faded but familiar. "There was a second set of terms."

Her breath caught. Their child's pact that she'd insisted they draw up, he'd retained it… all these years.

"I was to make you deliriously happy, Gillian," he murmured, reciting the words on that page he turned toward her. "*That* was the agreement."

"You always make me deliriously happy," she whispered.

"Mm-mm. *Forever*," he clarified. He took a step toward her. "The promise was forever."

Yes, because even as a small girl, she'd known she wanted to spend all her days with Colin Lockhart. Gillian turned a trembling palm up. "I still don't understand."

Those beloved green eyes traveled over her, and then he brought his hands up to cup her cheeks, framing her face as if she were the most cherished gift. "All that you asked for when we married was that I promise to make you laugh and smile every day, and I want that."

Gillian clutched a fist to her chest. What was he saying? Even as she knew... she was too afraid to hope. To believe.

"But you deserve so much more," he went on. "Someone to share your dreams and fight your dragons alongside you. Someone to build you up and then hold you close when you fall down, and I want that," he said, his voice an impassioned plea. His hands shook, and she felt that tremble all the way to where her heart swelled with every word he spoke.

He released her, and she wept inside for the loss of his touch.

Colin looked out at the sprawling green hills around them. "I spent the past twelve years missing you, Gillian." His throat moved quickly. He shifted his stare once more to her. "And the moment you left that inn, I knew one thing."

Her lip trembled, and she caught it between her teeth to steady it. "What was that?"

"I don't want to spend the rest of my days without you." He lowered his brow to hers. "I want forever with you, Gillian."

Tears blurred her vision, and she furiously blinked to clear them so she might see him. So she might convince herself that this was real.

"Marry me. Please. I cannot give you a title, and I'll only ever be a self-made, and—"

Sobbing, she threw herself into his arms, and his arms immediately came up around her, holding her tight. "Yes."

Colin buried his face in the curve of her shoulder. "And I've not finished. I've not mentioned the part that it is likely that we will have to live in Birmingham and—"

"Yes." She laughed through her tears, gripping his shoulders and squeezing. "Yes to marriage and yes to Birmingham and yes to our beginning anew somewhere else, together." Gillian tipped her face up and joined her mouth with his in a kiss that whispered at that new beginning.

Together.

EPILOGUE

WHEN GILLIAN HAD FIRST REENTERED his life, showing up his offices, she'd insisted she could help him find clever, competent staff, and the organization of his overall business.

She'd not lied.

And she'd not been wrong.

With her hands on her hips, Gillian fired off directives, ordering about the small army of servants filing about the room. The way she'd taken charge and commanded the group, she could have served as the model of a military general; one in perfect control of her men.

From where he stood at the front of his new Birmingham agency—or what would become his and O'Toole's new agency—Colin lounged a shoulder against the doorjamb and watched on, unobserved, as she worked.

His lips formed a wry grin. But why, then would any of the men he'd hired to oversee the transformation of the old, empty offices notice their employer, Colin, when there was a presence like Gillian in their midst.

Captivated. He could watch her all day. And following their

flight to Gretna Green a month earlier, that is how he spent a good deal of his time.

I cannot believe she is mine...

"If you would, please, just leave that there?" she was asking, the pair of stocky twins who now between the two of them, carried an enormous scroll desk. The two men, who, since they'd been hired a fortnight ago, would walk from one tip of Birmingham to the other and back again if she so commanded.

Of course, it certainly helped that Gillian didn't really order the men working for them about. That she was kind and polite, and didn't take it as her due that the men who'd been hired to set up the agency, were beholden in any way. She treated them as equals; teasing them, and speaking with them as she would anyone. In short, it was all the reasons he'd fallen in love with her all those years ago. As a boy, he'd known precisely the manner of special person that she was.

Gillian clapped. "That is splendid. I do appreciate all your help, Terry and Terrence."

The crimson-haired twins, each like images of the other, tugged their caps off simultaneously. "Is there anything else you required," they said in perfect unison.

"I—" Gillian's gaze snagged on Colin, and her entire face lit, the joy that filled her features, having the same dizzying effect it always did on his heart and head.

Smiling widely, he touched his fingers to his lips, and sent her a kiss.

"Why don't you gentlemen take a break. I see my husband has arrived."

The twins immediately spun and dropped a bow. "Mr. Lockhart."

"Terry. Terrence," he called back over the din of the construction.

"In fact," Gillian clapped her hands, instantly commanding the attention of the twelve men at work. "Why don't you all take a short rest?"

The men hurried to finish whatever task they saw to, and proceeded to file past Colin, and through the front door.

Straightening, Colin nodded, as each man passed.

Until he and Gillian... were, at last, alone.

Holding her palm out, she came toward him. "Dear heart."

"My heart," he returned with their familiar greeting.

If his brothers could see him now, he thought wryly.

Going up on tiptoe, she tipped her head back for a kiss. He brushed his mouth over hers.

Those tantalizing lips formed a perfect pink moue. "I daresay I expected more—"

He kissed her once more; teasing her lips open and sliding his tongue against hers in that perfect dance they'd practiced so well this past month, and one he would never tire of.

When he drew back, she sighed. A dazed little sparkle glimmered in her eyes.

"Better?" he teased, flicking her nose.

"Very much so, husband." She stilled; her gaze moving over his face. "What is it?"

Of course she could see there was more. They'd always had an uncanny ability to sense the emotion within one another.

"I've received word. Lord Barber was killed in a duel."

Her lips parted. "Was he?"

"He arrived drunk to the field and…and… met the fate he deserved at the other end of Lord Lincoln's dueling pistol." And never had he so relished another man's death.

Gillian hugged her arms around her middle and wandered off. "Is it wrong I feel no remorse at his having met his end?"

Colin stalked over, and put himself in the path she'd taken away from him. "You are entitled to feel absolutely anything and everything you feel, unapologetically, Gillian. He was a black-hearted cur, and the world is better without him. As he wronged you so, there was undoubtedly others, and there would undoubtedly be more."

"I have had that thought, too. Many times. How many other women…and how many did not have someone like you to be there in the aftermath?"

The sadness in her voice caused his chest to ache with the pain she carried, when all he wanted, was for her each day to be filled only with laughter and happiness.

She shook her head. "I have given him enough of my life, Colin.

He is dead, and he is gone. This day and for every day."

God, how he loved her. He palmed her cheeks once more. "You are... magnificent, Gillian Lockhart."

And just like that, her eyes reflected only joy, light, and love.

Taking her by the hand, he led her deeper into the room, surveying the layout of the room that, with the desks, filing cases, and seating, was actually beginning to look like an agency. "You have done...a splendid job."

She beamed and with her spare palm, patted at her flyaway golden curls. "I have, haven't I?"

"Well, you did promise as much, when you first came to see me in London. You were indeed, correct. About the offices..." He stopped beside the broad, mahogany scroll desk that would be his at this new place. "...and more."

Her lashes dipped. "You have a secret."

Seating himself on the edge of his desk, Colin drew Gillian between the vee of his legs. "You are going to be a detective. That is all to it. And you shall put me and O'Toole to shame with your skill and—"

Laughing, she swatted at him.

"There were other terms to our arrangement, love."

Her brow dipped. "Other?"

"A circus."

Her lips mouthed that word, and confusion puckered the little space between her eyes, and then she stilled. Laughing once more, she leaned close. "Ah, yes, the menagerie and all the friends. You remember that."

He brushed a single golden curl back behind her ear. "I remember everything where you are concerned, Gillian Lockhart," he said solemnly.

Her lips trembled. "I love you."

"I love you, and want us to have those wedding festivities you dreamed of for us...with archery and games and the friends and the family you rightly predicted we'd have."

Her breath caught on a little gasp. "In...deed?"

Colin cupped her right cheek, and she leaned into his touch. "Indeed. Not the parents who wronged us," Neither his father.

Nor her parents whom she'd vowed to never again see. "but the siblings who built us up and made us better…and the friends of yours whom I've still yet to meet."

Tears glimmered in her eyes, and he made a soothing sound. "Hey, what is this love."

"It is just," she wiped at those tears, until he saw to the task of brushing away her sadness, himself. "I've avoided talking to or seeing Honoria. Because I didn't know how to face her and I've missed her," Her breath caught on a little sob, and he drew her into his arms, cradling her close. "I want her there. And Genevieve and Cedric and their new babe. And Francesca. I want you to finally meet her, and—"

"And I'll meet them all, love. They'll all be there. At our *Mariage Grand Cirque*."

Colin and Gillian's laughter melded and blended, and he took her in his arms once more.

The End

OTHER BOOKS IN THE HEART OF A DUKE SERIES BY CHRISTI CALDWELL

TO TEMPT A SCOUNDREL
Book 15 in the "Heart of a Duke" Series by Christi Caldwell

Never trust a gentleman…

Once before, Lady Alice Winterbourne trusted her heart to an honorable, respectable man… only to be jilted in the scandal of the Season. Longing for an escape from all the whispers and humiliation, Alice eagerly accepts an invitation to her friend's house party. In the country, she hopes to find some peace from the embarrassment left in London… Unfortunately, she finds her former betrothed and his new bride in attendance.

Never love a lady…

Lord Rhys Brookfield has no interest in marriage. Ever. He's worked quite hard at building both his fortune and his reputation as a rogue—and intends to enjoy all that they can offer him. That is if his match-making mother will stop pairing him with prospective brides. When Rhys and Alice meet, sparks flare. But with every new encounter, their first impressions of one another are challenged and an unlikely friendship is forged.

Desperate, Rhys proposes a pretend courtship, one meant to spite Alice's former betrothed and prevent any matchmaking attempts toward Rhys. What neither expects is that a pretense can become so much more. Or that a burning passion can heal… and hurt.

Beguiled by a Baron
Book 14 in the "Heart of a Duke" Series by Christi Caldwell

A Lady with a Secret... Partially deaf, with a birthmark marring her face, Bridget Hamilton is content with her life, even if she's been cast out of her family. But her peaceful existence—expanding her mind with her study of rare books—is threatened with an ultimatum from her evil brother—steal a valuable book or give up her son. Bridget has no choice; her son is her world.

A Lord with a Purpose... Vail Basingstoke, Baron Chilton is known throughout London as the Bastard Baron. After battling at Waterloo, he establishes himself as the foremost dealer in rare books and builds a fortune, determined to never be like the self-serving duke who sired him. He devotes his life to growing his fortune to care for his illegitimate siblings, also fathered by the duke. The chance to sell a highly coveted book for a financial windfall is his only thought.

Two Paths Collide... When Bridget masquerades as the baron's newest housekeeper, he's hopelessly intrigued by her quick wit and her skill with antique tomes. Wary from having his heart broken in the past, it should be easy enough to keep Bridget at arm's length, yet desire for her dogs his steps. As they spend time in each other's company, understanding for life grows as does love, but when Bridget's integrity is called into question, Vail's world is shattered—as is his heart again. Now Bridget and Vail will have to overcome the horrendous secrets and lies between them to grasp a love—and life—together.

To Enchant a Wicked Duke
Book 13 in the "Heart of a Duke" Series by Christi Caldwell

A Devil in Disguise

Years ago, when Nick Tallings, the recent Duke of Huntly, watched his family destroyed at the hands of a merciless nobleman, he vowed revenge. But his efforts had been futile, as his enemy, Lord Rutland is without weakness.

Until now…

With his rival finally happily married, Nick is able to set his ruthless scheme into motion. His plot hinges upon Lord Rutland's innocent, empty-headed sister-in-law, Justina Barrett. Nick will ruin her, marry her, and then leave her brokenhearted.

A Lady Dreaming of Love

From the moment Justina Barrett makes her Come Out, she is labeled a Diamond. Even with her ruthless father determined to sell her off to the highest bidder, Justina never gives up on her hope for a good, honorable gentleman who values her wit more than her looks.

A Not-So-Chance Meeting

Nick's ploy to ensnare Justina falls neatly into place in the streets of London. With each carefully orchestrated encounter, he slips further and further inside the lady's heart, never anticipating that Justina, with her quick wit and strength, will break down his own defenses. As Nick's plans begins to unravel, he's left to determine which is more important—Justina's love or his vow for vengeance. But can Justina ever forgive the duke who deceived her?

One Winter with a Baron
Book 12 in the "Heart of a Duke" Series by Christi Caldwell

A clever spinster:
Content with her spinster lifestyle, Miss Sybil Cunning wants to prove that a future as an unmarried woman is the only life for her. As a bluestocking who values hard, empirical data, Sybil needs help with her research. Nolan Pratt, Baron Webb, one of society's most scandalous rakes, is the perfect gentleman to help her. After all, he inspires fear in proper mothers and desire within their daughters.

A notorious rake:
Society may be aware of Nolan Pratt, Baron's Webb's wicked ways, but what he has carefully hidden is his miserable handling of his family's finances. When Sybil presents him the opportunity to earn much-needed funds, he can't refuse.

A winter to remember:
However, what begins as a business arrangement becomes something more and with every meeting, Sybil slips inside his heart. Can this clever woman look beneath the veneer of a coldhearted rake to see the man Nolan truly is?

To Redeem a Rake
Book 11 in the "Heart of a Duke" Series by Christi Caldwell

He's spent years scandalizing society.

Now, this rake must change his ways.

Society's most infamous scoundrel, Daniel Winterbourne, the Earl of Montfort, has been promised a small fortune if he can relinquish his wayward, carousing lifestyle. And behaving means he must also help find a respectable companion for his youngest sister—someone who will guide her and whom she can emulate. However, Daniel knows no such woman. But when he encounters a childhood friend, Daniel believes she may just be the answer to all of his problems.

Having been secretly humiliated by an unscrupulous blackguard years earlier, Miss Daphne Smith dreams of finding work at Ladies of Hope, an institution that provides an education for disabled women. With her sordid past and a disfigured leg, few opportunities arise for a woman such as she. Knowing Daniel's history, she wishes to avoid him, but working for his sister is exactly the stepping stone she needs.

Their attraction intensifies as Daniel and Daphne grow closer, preparing his sister for the London Season. But Daniel must resist his desire for a woman tarnished by scandal while Daphne is reminded of the boy she once knew. Can society's most notorious rake redeem his reputation and become the man Daphne deserves?

To Woo A Widow
Book 10 in the "Heart of a Duke" Series by Christi Caldwell

They see a brokenhearted widow.

She's far from shattered.
Lady Philippa Winston is never marrying again. After her late husband's cruelty that she kept so well hidden, she has no desire to search for love.

Years ago, Miles Brookfield, the Marquess of Guilford, made a frivolous vow he never thought would come to fruition—he promised to marry his mother's goddaughter if he was unwed by the age of thirty. Now, to his dismay, he's faced with honoring that pledge. But when he encounters the beautiful and intriguing Lady Philippa, Miles knows his true path in life. It's up to him to break down every belief Philippa carries about gentlemen, proving that not only is love real, but that he is the man deserving of her sheltered heart.

Will Philippa let down her guard and allow Miles to woo a widow in desperate need of his love?

The Lure of a Rake
Book 9 in the "Heart of a Duke" Series by Christi Caldwell

A Lady Dreaming of Love

Lady Genevieve Farendale has a scandalous past. Jilted at the altar years earlier and exiled by her family, she's now returned to London to prove she can be a proper lady. Even though she's not given up on the hope of marrying for love, she's wary of trusting again. Then she meets Cedric Falcot, the Marquess of St. Albans whose seductive ways set her heart aflutter. But with her sordid history, Genevieve knows a rake can also easily destroy her.

An Unlikely Pairing

What begins as a chance encounter between Cedric and Genevieve becomes something more. As they continue to meet, passions stir. But with Genevieve's hope for true love, she fears Cedric will be unable to give up his wayward lifestyle. After all, Cedric has spent years protecting his heart, and keeping everyone out. Slowly, she chips away at all the walls he's built, but when he falters, Genevieve can't offer him redemption. Now, it's up to Cedric to prove to Genevieve that the love of a man is far more powerful than the lure of a rake.

To Trust a Rogue
Book 8 in the "Heart of a Duke" Series by Christi Caldwell

A rogue

Marcus, the Viscount Wessex has carefully crafted the image of rogue and charmer for Polite Society. Under that façade, however, dwells a man whose dreams were shattered almost eight years earlier by a young lady who captured his heart, pledged her love, and then left him, with nothing more than a curt note.

A widow

Eight years earlier, faced with no other choice, Mrs. Eleanor Collins, fled London and the only man she ever loved, Marcus, Viscount Wessex. She has now returned to serve as a companion for her elderly aunt with a daughter in tow. Even though they're next door neighbors, there is little reason for her to move in the same circles as Marcus, just in case, she vows to avoid him, for he reminds her of all she lost when she left.

Reunited

As their paths continue to cross, Marcus finds his desire for Eleanor just as strong, but he learned long ago she's not to be trusted. He will offer her a place in his bed, but not anything more. Only, Eleanor has no interest in this new, roguish man. The more time they spend together, the protective wall they've constructed to keep the other out, begin to break. With all the betrayals and secrets between them, Marcus has to open his heart again. And Eleanor must decide if it's ever safe to trust a rogue.

To Wed His Christmas Lady
Book 7 in the "Heart of a Duke" Series by Christi Caldwell

She's longing to be loved:

Lady Cara Falcot has only served one purpose to her loathsome father—to increase his power through a marriage to the future Duke of Billingsley. As such, she's built protective walls about her heart, and presents an icy facade to the world around her. Journeying home from her finishing school for the Christmas holidays, Cara's carriage is stranded during a winter storm. She's forced to tarry at a ramshackle inn, where she immediately antagonizes another patron—William.

He's avoiding his duty in favor of one last adventure:

William Hargrove, the Marquess of Grafton has wanted only one thing in life—to avoid the future match his parents would have him make to a cold, duke's daughter. He's returning home from a blissful eight years of traveling the world to see to his responsibilities. But when a winter storm interrupts his trip and lands him at a falling-down inn, he's forced to share company with a commanding Lady Cara who initially reminds him exactly of the woman he so desperately wants to avoid.

A Christmas snowstorm ushers in the spirit of the season:

At the holiday time, these two people who despise each other due to first perceptions are offered renewed beginnings and fresh starts. As this gruff stranger breaks down the walls she's built about herself, Cara has to determine whether she can truly open her heart to trusting that any man is capable of good and that she herself is capable of love. And William has to set aside all previous thoughts he's carried of the polished ladies like Cara, to be the man to show her that love.

The Heart of a Scoundrel
Book 6 in the "Heart of a Duke" Series by Christi Caldwell

Ruthless, wicked, and dark, the Marquess of Rutland rouses terror in the breast of ladies and nobleman alike. All Edmund wants in life is power. After he was publically humiliated by his one love Lady Margaret, he vowed vengeance, using Margaret's niece, as his pawn. Except, he's thwarted by another, more enticing target—Miss Phoebe Barrett.

Miss Phoebe Barrett knows precisely the shame she's been born to. Because her father is a shocking letch she's learned to form her own opinions on a person's worth. After a chance meeting with the Marquess of Rutland, she is captivated by the mysterious man. He, too, is a victim of society's scorn, but the more encounters she has with Edmund, the more she knows there is powerful depth and emotion to the jaded marquess.

The lady wreaks havoc on Edmund's plans for revenge and he finds he wants Phoebe, at all costs. As she's drawn into the darkness of his world, Phoebe risks being destroyed by Edmund's ruthlessness. And Phoebe who desires love at all costs, has to determine if she can ever truly trust the heart of a scoundrel.

TO LOVE A LORD
Book 5 in the "Heart of a Duke" Series by Christi Caldwell

All she wants is security:

The last place finishing school instructor Mrs. Jane Munroe belongs, is in polite Society. Vowing to never wed, she's been scuttled around from post to post. Now she finds herself in the Marquess of Waverly's household. She's never met a nobleman she liked, and when she meets the pompous, arrogant marquess, she remembers why. But soon, she discovers Gabriel is unlike any gentleman she's ever known.

All he wants is a companion for his sister:

What Gabriel finds himself with instead, is a fiery spirited, bespectacled woman who entices him at every corner and challenges his age-old vow to never trust his heart to a woman. But…there is something suspicious about his sister's companion. And he is determined to find out just what it is.

All they need is each other:

As Gabriel and Jane confront the truth of their feelings, the lies and secrets between them begin to unravel. And Jane is left to decide whether or not it is ever truly safe to love a lord.

Loved By a Duke
Book 4 in the "Heart of a Duke" Series by Christi Caldwell

For ten years, Lady Daisy Meadows has been in love with Auric, the Duke of Crawford. Ever since his gallant rescue years earlier, Daisy knew she was destined to be his Duchess. Unfortunately, Auric sees her as his best friend's sister and nothing more. But perhaps, if she can manage to find the fabled heart of a duke pendant, she will win over the heart of her duke.

Auric, the Duke of Crawford enjoys Daisy's company. The last thing he is interested in however, is pursuing a romance with a woman he's known since she was in leading strings. This season, Daisy is turning up in the oddest places and he cannot help but notice that she is no longer a girl. But Auric wouldn't do something as foolhardy as to fall in love with Daisy. He couldn't. Not with the guilt he carries over his past sins… Not when he has no right to her heart…But perhaps, just perhaps, she can forgive the past and trust that he'd forever cherish her heart—but will she let him?

THE LOVE OF A ROGUE
Book 3 in the "Heart of a Duke" Series by Christi Caldwell

Lady Imogen Moore hasn't had an easy time of it since she made her Come Out. With her betrothed, a powerful duke breaking it off to wed her sister, she's become the *tons* favorite piece of gossip. Never again wanting to experience the pain of a broken heart, she's resolved to make a match with a polite, respectable gentleman. The last thing she wants is another reckless rogue.

Lord Alex Edgerton has a problem. His brother, tired of Alex's carousing has charged him with chaperoning their remaining, unwed sister about *ton* events. Shopping? No, thank you. Attending the theatre? He'd rather be at Forbidden Pleasures with a scantily clad beauty upon his lap. The task of *chaperone* becomes even more of a bother when his sister drags along her dearest friend, Lady Imogen to social functions. The last thing he wants in his life is a young, innocent English miss.

Except, as Alex and Imogen are thrown together, passions flare and Alex comes to find he not only wants Imogen in his bed, but also in his heart. Yet now he must convince Imogen to risk all, on the heart of a rogue.

More Than a Duke
Book 2 in the "Heart of a Duke" Series by Christi Caldwell

Polite Society doesn't take Lady Anne Adamson seriously. However, Anne isn't just another pretty young miss. When she discovers her father betrayed her mother's love and her family descended into poverty, Anne comes up with a plan to marry a respectable, powerful, and honorable gentleman—a man nothing like her philandering father.

Armed with the heart of a duke pendant, fabled to land the wearer a duke's heart, she decides to enlist the aid of the notorious Harry, 6th Earl of Stanhope. A scoundrel with a scandalous past, he is the last gentleman she'd ever wed…however, his reputation marks him the perfect man to school her in the art of seduction so she might ensnare the illustrious Duke of Crawford.

Harry, the Earl of Stanhope is a jaded, cynical rogue who lives for his own pleasures. Having been thrown over by the only woman he ever loved so she could wed a duke, he's not at all surprised when Lady Anne approaches him with her scheme to capture another duke's affection. He's come to appreciate that all women are in fact greedy, title-grasping, self-indulgent creatures. And with Anne's history of grating on his every last nerve, she is the last woman he'd ever agree to school in the art of seduction. Only his friendship with the lady's sister compels him to help.

What begins as a pretend courtship, born of lessons on seduction, becomes something more leaving Anne to decide if she can give her heart to a reckless rogue, and Harry must decide if he's willing to again trust in a lady's love.

For Love of the Duke
First Full-Length Book in the "Heart of a Duke" Series
by Christi Caldwell

After the tragic death of his wife, Jasper, the 8th Duke of Bainbridge buried himself away in the dark cold walls of his home, Castle Blackwood. When he's coaxed out of his self-imposed exile to attend the amusements of the Frost Fair, his life is irrevocably changed by his fateful meeting with Lady Katherine Adamson.

With her tight brown ringlets and silly white-ruffled gowns, Lady Katherine Adamson has found her dance card empty for two Seasons. After her father's passing, Katherine learned the unreliability of men, and is determined to depend on no one, except herself. Until she meets Jasper…

In a desperate bid to avoid a match arranged by her family, Katherine makes the Duke of Bainbridge a shocking proposition—one that he accepts.

Only, as Katherine begins to love Jasper, she finds the arrangement agreed upon is not enough. And Jasper is left to decide if protecting his heart is more important than fighting for Katherine's love.

In Need of a Duke
*A Prequel Novella to "The Heart of a Duke" Series
by Christi Caldwell*

In Need of a Duke: (Author's Note: This is a prequel novella to "The Heart of a Duke" series by Christi Caldwell. It was originally available in "The Heart of a Duke" Collection and is now being published as an individual novella.

It features a new prologue and epilogue.

Years earlier, a gypsy woman passed to Lady Aldora Adamson and her friends a heart pendant that promised them each the heart of a duke.

Now, a young lady, with her family facing ruin and scandal, Lady Aldora doesn't have time for mythical stories about cheap baubles. She needs to save her sisters and brother by marrying a titled gentleman with wealth and power to his name. She sets her bespectacled sights upon the Marquess of St. James.

Turned out by his father after a tragic scandal, Lord Michael Knightly has grown into a powerful, but self-made man. With the whispers and stares that still follow him, he would rather be anywhere but London…

Until he meets Lady Aldora, a young woman who mistakes him for his brother, the Marquess of St. James. The connection between Aldora and Michael is immediate and as they come to know one another, Aldora's feelings for Michael war with her sisterly responsibilities. With her family's dire situation, a man of Michael's scandalous past will never do.

Ultimately, Aldora must choose between her responsibilities as a sister and her love for Michael.

BIOGRAPHY

Christi Caldwell is the bestselling author of historical romance novels set in the Regency era. Christi blames Judith McNaught's "Whitney, My Love," for luring her into the world of historical romance. While sitting in her graduate school apartment at the University of Connecticut, Christi decided to set aside her notes and try her hand at writing romance. She believes the most perfect heroes and heroines have imperfections and rather enjoys tormenting them before crafing a well-deserved happily ever after!

When Christi isn't writing the stories of flawed heroes and heroines, she can be found in her Southern Connecticut home chasing around her eight-year-old son, and caring for twin princesses-in-training!

Visit *www.christicaldwellauthor.com* to learn more about what Christi is working on, or join her on Facebook at Christi Caldwell Author, and Twitter @ChristiCaldwell

Printed in Great Britain
by Amazon